Kitty

William Corlett

William Corlett

CORGI BOOKS

KITTY

A CORGI BOOK 0552 550787

Published in Great Britain by Corgi Books,
an imprint of Random House Children's Books

This edition published 2004

1 3 5 7 9 10 8 6 4 2

Set in Bembo by Palimpsest Book Production Limited, Polmont, Stirlingshire

Corgi Books are published by Random House Children's Books,
61–63 Uxbridge Road, London W5 5SA,
a division of The Random House Group Ltd,
in Australia by Random House Australia (Pty) Ltd,
20 Alfred Street, Milsons Point, Sydney, NSW 2061, Australia,
in New Zealand by Random House New Zealand Ltd,
18 Poland Road, Glenfield, Auckland 10, New Zealand,
and in South Africa by Random House (Pty) Ltd,
Endulini, 5A Jubilee Road, Parktown 2193, South Africa

THE RANDOM HOUSE GROUP Limited Reg. No. 954009
www.kidsatrandomhouse.co.uk

A CIP catalogue record for this book is available from the British Library.

Printed and bound in Great Britain by Cox and Wyman Ltd, Reading, Berkshire

For
Joanna, David and Bryn
and for
Bailey,
bravest of dogs

There is a range of low rolling hills to the south of the mountains called the Sierra Nevada, in southern Spain. This is a wild, desolate land; baked by a near African sun during the summer months and cold enough for snow once in a while in winter. On their southern side the hills drop in long, folding valleys – like the pleats on a Spanish skirt – down to a restless, sometimes stormy sea. The people of the coast are mainly farmers now. They grow vegetables in vast plastic greenhouses. Vegetables that will end up on the shelves of supermarkets all over Europe. Your Little Gem lettuce, your green pepper, your tomato or cucumber or courgette – any one of these could have come from this place.

Inland, however, higher up in the hills, the ancient world of Spain is still to be found. Here whitewashed villages swelter and swoon under a noontide sun and the owl and the bat inhabit the dark.

It is a harsh landscape, rocky and parched during the summer months when springs turn to a trickle as the searching sun beats down and even the birds are silent, hiding in whatever shade they can find. In winter when the rains fall it is a different climate; grim, inhospitable and surprisingly cold for the fox and the rat and all the other secret animals of the wild.

This foreign place then is Kitty's world and the world of Bailey, her beloved companion.

And this is their story; a true adventure of two dogs, told to me by people who knew some of it and by Kitty, who remembers it all.

Chapter One

'Cat!'

'Where?'

'Went straight up that wall!'

Those were the first words I ever heard Joanna and David say that I really understood. Before, their words had just been a muddle of strange sounds to me. Then, suddenly, that day I knew what they were saying. But at the time can you imagine how disgusted I felt? To be mistaken for a cat! Me! I hate cats!

I was with Dog and he laughed. He was used to their funny language and understood them long before I did. Dog had been around. That's what he used to tell me: 'I've been around, Little!' He called me Little in those days, although he was no bigger than I was really. 'I've been around, Little. I know things. That's why you need me . . .'

In those early days he was always telling me that I needed him. And, of course, he was right.

But I suppose I'd better begin at the beginning . . .

Chapter Two

I don't remember my mother very well; I have just a vague picture in my mind of someone warm and terribly thin.

I was one of a litter of seven, and because there was so little food that spring she had hardly enough milk for us all and soon became very weak.

I had three brothers and three sisters and we lived in an old box outside a house by the big water.

My mother was no more than a pup herself. She didn't really know our father and I don't think she liked him very much. She told us girls that when it was the time of year when we would be ready to have pups we should hide from the dogs. She said having pups was very difficult and not worth the trouble. I thought that sounded as though she wished she hadn't had us — which wasn't very nice, considering we were there and hadn't chosen to be and we were her family whether she liked it or not.

My mother and I didn't really get on and, if I'm honest, that was my fault. I thought she didn't love us enough. When we were feeding she would pull away from us. We were always hungry and yet she didn't like us taking her milk. She used to snap and once she bit me quite badly. I think she was sorry afterwards, but I resented it. I said she was a bad mother and I called her mean names.

But now, now that I'm older, now that I know how hard life can be if a dog doesn't start out in a lucky place, now I realize how difficult it was for her and I wish . . . I wish I could see her and tell her that I understand and that I forgive her and that I'm sorry I complained so much.

But I never will, of course. Not now. I'm not even sure where she lives now. The journey has been so long that I don't think I could find my way back even if I wanted to – which I don't. Besides, I don't know that any of them would be alive if I did. But sometimes I still think about Mother and I wonder what her life was like before us. Did she have fun? Did she . . . love a dog? Where was she born? Who were her brothers and sisters? It is sad not to know your family's history. That's what Fanny told me once. Of course, she can say such things because she knows all about herself and where she came from and who her family were. I think sometimes she enjoys reminding me that I don't. She says that I don't belong anywhere. Not really . . .

But even Fanny has grown to like me, I think, with the passing of time – but that is all way in the future of this story, anyway, and I mustn't jump ahead.

So . . .

My history started in a dirty, smelly yard, in a cardboard box. A human used to throw out scraps for us and after we were weaned that's what we lived on.

Our number was quite soon reduced to four.

One brother was hit by a car on the road that lay just behind the house and was very busy and noisy and terrifying to us all. I don't know why he went on the road. I think he was chasing something. The car that hit him didn't stop. Maybe the driver didn't know that he'd killed him. Or maybe he didn't care.

Then one of our sisters died. She was the last to be born and she had never been strong. We others avoided her. Being weak was unlucky and we didn't want her bad luck visiting us.

But it was the second brother to go who really interested me. This happened when we had been alive for about a quarter of a year. He used to wander further than the rest of us. He would come racing back with stories about how wet the big water was and how huge the world. He said there were humans right along the beach and that there was a place where they sat outside and had food on plates. He said that sometimes they threw scraps to him. It all sounded like a big story to me. But it was true that he seemed to be better fed than the rest of us. I asked him where this place was where the humans threw scraps. But he wouldn't tell me. I think he was afraid that I would get in his way.

Then one day he didn't come home. Our human always threw out our food just as the sun was disappearing over the hill. We were always there, waiting. It was the highlight of our day. But on this evening my brother didn't come back for his food and we none of us saw him again.

How odd now to remember that; I think things in life happen over and over again. Maybe that's the way we have a chance of learning from them.

But at the time all I thought was: He's staying at the place where he gets scraps off the plates. He's no fool. He gets better food there than we ever have.

Two of the other pups were really ill by now. I think they had 'dis-ease'. Mother and the other two just lay around all the time in what little shade they could find. Each day the sun was getting hotter and they couldn't be bothered to play. They didn't even go down to the edge of the big water any more. I think, looking back, that all of them had 'lost the will to live' – well, that's what Dog told me had happened when I described it to him later.

But I hadn't 'lost the will'. In fact, quite the reverse. I didn't want my world to be no bigger than a yard, or my life no better than a scrap. I decided that as I'd been born I should go out and live. Somehow, even then, I knew that life could be good; but that it was up to me to go and make it so. And so one night after a particularly bad supper when the others were all curled up near the box – there wasn't room for all of us in it now and Mother used it for herself – I went down the beach and turned my back on the big water . . .

After the heat of the day there was a little breeze blowing and it felt cooler away from the dusty yard. The air was fresher there and I could smell strange, sweet, herby scents. Behind the village the land rose up through a broad, shallow valley towards distant rolling hills. Beyond the tops of these hills I could see the tips of jagged mountains, capped with snow. The sun was setting on this scene and the light was misting and smudging towards dark. As I watched I saw the lights of a village halfway up the valley gradually twinkle into life and hang there in the gloaming like a scatter of jewels on the dark earth.

I knew then what a big world was all around me waiting to be discovered and I didn't want to stay in a dusty, dirty yard for the rest of my life.

I wanted to go on an adventure.

Chapter Three

My fur is the colour of honey. Mother's was darker, a rich red-gold, and my brothers and sisters were mainly mottled; brown, black and gold. But mine is all one colour: sweet, golden honey-coloured. I am actually rather proud of my fur.

Mother must once have been very pretty and I don't think I'm being vain when I say that I take after her. I know this because the house where we lived had a glass door into the yard and I could see my reflection in it and the reflection of all the other pups and of Mother.

I only mention this because Dog was so completely different to me. His fur was black but he had white socks, a white bib, a white nose and a stripe of white right up his snout and over onto his shoulders. The black was the blackest of blacks and the white so very white. The first time I saw him . . . I think I loved him at once. I didn't tell him, of course. Mother had warned me about that. But, oh! I did like the look of him.

And I think I knew at once that he also liked the look of me. He kept staring at me, which I found rather alarming. So I turned tail and ran.

After I'd gone a little way I looked back to see if he was following me. But he wasn't. He was standing exactly where he had been when I first saw him. He had one front paw raised and his head was tilted to the side. He was staring at me. His mouth was slightly open and I could hear his breath panting. I also noticed that his tail — which was stubby and curved and was flashed with white on the tip — was wagging. I thought he looked particularly silly and turned my back on him. But then, later, I had to look back again because he still wasn't following me.

In fact he seemed to have got stuck to the ground. He hadn't moved at all. He just stood there, staring, with his head on one side.

In the end I had to go back to him. I was learning a very important lesson. Dog waited for me to come to him. Or, to put it another way, I was always waiting for him to come to me but he very rarely did. In the early days I used to think that was because he didn't really like me. But later, when I got to know him — and I got to know him almost as well as I know myself — I realized that he didn't come to me because he liked me too much. He liked me so much that he was afraid I wouldn't want him. I wish that from the beginning he'd had more confidence. But that was Dog. He was the bravest dog ever. He was the kindest. He was even quite good looking. But he had no confidence at all about me. I had to really show him how much I liked him. And sometimes I wanted him to do that to me instead. I wanted him to run after me instead of always standing there just behind me, staring and panting and wagging.

So that first time I saw him was to be the first of the many, many times that I ran up to him and skipped and jumped in front of him and barked and . . . egged him on, really.

He barked back then and ran at me and I ran away and he ran after me and we dodged and turned and had a good game. But I had to start it all. I had to egg him on. I had to show that I wanted him to chase me. He always thought he was faster than I was. But that's only because on that first time I let him think that. I didn't use all my speed. I never did when we were playing together. I'm sure I could have outrun him – if I'd wanted to.

We chased quite a long way along the beach, splashing in and out of the shallows of the big water and kicking up sand.

We came to a place where there were trees and a few shrubs and bushes and long coarse grass. There was fresh water in a narrow channel. He said we were lucky, later in the year the sun would dry it up. I don't know how he knew things. Being older, I suppose. When we'd lapped our fill he showed me how to dig a nest in the earth with the front paws and how to push the soil into a wall with the back ones, so that eventually there was quite a hollow to lie in. He did this beneath the branches of a sweet-smelling bush and when we lay down to sleep I thought it was the most perfect bed I had ever known.

We curled up next to each other and I could feel his body breathing and I could smell him and he was warm.

'Where were you going?' he asked me.

'When?'

'When we met.'

'I don't know.'

'You can come with me, if you like.'

'Why?'

'Two dogs are safer than one,' he replied.

We didn't know about names then. None of my brothers and sisters had been given a name and I never heard the human call my mother anything at all. In fact, I don't think she was ever spoken to by any humans, apart from sometimes being shouted at and once, when we were very small, a boy came and stroked her. But Mother didn't trust him, so she snapped at him and made him run away.

Dog didn't have a name either when I met him. So I just called him Dog for quite a long time and he called me Little.

It was only when we got to the magic garden that we became Kitty – that's me – and Bailey.

Chapter Four

We stayed by the water channel until, as Dog said it would, the water ran dry.

He knew how to get into a big bin at the back of the table place. I think maybe the table place was where my brother had gone to get scraps off the humans. We didn't bother with that, really. We didn't need to. Dog knew where all the waste food was thrown away at the end of the evening and we used to go there after dark. Most nights there was quite a feast. Bits of bone, fish heads, bread and scraps of gristle and fat. I don't know why my mother hadn't taken us all there. It was far better than the human's scraps back in the yard.

But one night I got a fish bone stuck in the roof of my mouth. When we went back to the nest I tried to suck it away, but I couldn't move it — in fact I think I made it worse. The following morning my mouth was very sore. For a couple of days I couldn't eat anything and I started to feel weak. Eventually I became hot and drowsy and my body ached all over as though I'd been kicked.

Dog stayed with me all the time. He brought water on his tongue and when my mouth was open he licked the inside of my mouth, where the bone was stuck. He would run to the channel, bring water – it was no more than his damp tongue really, but it was cooled by the water – then he'd lick the roof of my mouth. I didn't really like him doing that, but I was too weak to prevent it. Where the bone had stuck into the roof of my mouth was all swollen and my breath smelled bad.

On the third morning when Dog was doing his licking the swelling burst and he got horrible, smelling pus on his tongue. He licked it all away and then went behind the bush and I heard him being sick.

After that I started to get better.

'You saved my life,' I told him later. We were at the channel, lapping. The water was very low now and it tasted of soil. But after being so ill, I was very thirsty. 'You saved my life,' I said again.

'Well!' he replied, with a gruff bark. 'Didn't want to lose you. Two dogs are safer than one.'

'What will we do when the water goes?' I asked him that night.

'Find other water,' he replied.

We were lying back to back in the nest and he was busy scratching a flea behind his ear.

'Where?' I asked.

'How would I know, till we find it?'

'Are you cross?'

'Go to sleep, Little,' he growled.

He wasn't cross, of course. He was worried. Worried about how we'd survive. Dog worried all the time about how we'd survive. The following morning when I woke he told me he'd made a plan. When I heard what he'd decided, it was so frightening that I almost wavered, almost wished I'd never left Mother in the dusty yard.

'We're going to have to cross the road,' he said.

I was appalled. 'Why?' I gasped.

'The summer sun here scorches the earth. You can't stand on the sand for fear of burning your feet. Even the big water gets warm. But more importantly there's not enough drinking water here. I've seen dogs lapping the big water and then going crazy – because of the salt. But up the valley the humans have places full of growing stuff. To make the stuff grow they squirt fresh, good water all the time. Plenty of water. Plenty of shade. We'll catch our food and drink their water . . . it'll be fine.'

'What will we catch?' I asked, doubting his every word. It didn't sound fine to me.

'Rat!' he said. 'We'll eat rat.'

'Thank you very much!' I said. I hoped he would notice the sarcasm, but he was too busy thinking.

'The humans make the growing places out of a thick stuff you can see through. We'll dig our way under this stuff and get inside . . .'

'But won't it be even hotter inside?' I protested.

'We'll get the water there and live somewhere else . . .'

'I like it here . . .'

'Little. We can't stay here.'

I think it was then that I started to dream of reaching a place where Dog and I could live in safety and in peace. I was dreaming of the magic garden of course, but I didn't know I was at the time.

'But first,' I heard him say, 'we have to cross the road.' And his voice was more serious, more chilling than ever before.

Chapter Five

He said it would be best to set out in the early morning because there weren't so many cars and lorries. He woke me when the sun was just beginning to edge up over the rim of the earth. We couldn't even see it, because of the hills that surrounded us. But the dark was getting thinner and there was a fine mist hanging low over the land.

We went first to the channel. There was only a trickle of water running and we had to scoop it into our mouths with our front paws. It was horrible. It tasted far worse than just muddy now; bitter and foul.

'What is it?' I asked, spitting it out of my mouth.

'Salt,' he said. 'The water's gone salt. Humans use so much of it that they've sucked the land dry and now the sea is filling up all the springs.'

It can be quite tiring living with a very clever dog. They know so much. Sometimes I think that Dog knew too much. It can't be good for a brain to be so full. We didn't need to know *why* the water tasted foul; it was obvious that it did without knowing the reason. But there! That was Dog! He was the cleverest I'm ever likely to know and I loved him all the more for that.

I was sorry to leave our nest under the sweet-smelling

bush. It had been our first home and so much had happened there.

'Don't look sad, Little. What's wrong?' he asked.

'I liked it here. This is where we were first together.'

'We'll always be together,' he growled.

And I believed him.

The road is very wide. I'd only ever once before been to look at it. Maybe because my brother was killed on it I thought it was an evil, unlucky place. But Dog said he'd been across often. I actually think he found it quite exciting. Much later in my story I used to see him chasing cars. Really! He would race along beside them, snapping at their spinning wheels. Frightened the life out of me! When he did that I used to close my eyes and hold my breath. Then, afterwards, when he came back to me, panting and with his eyes shining with excitement, I'd be really cross with him. 'D'you want to get killed?' I'd say. 'Like my brother got killed!' But Dog would just sit and scratch behind his ear and grin at me. Oh! He could be so . . . careless. He didn't stop to think. What good is a brain full of knowing if you don't stop to think? He sometimes got me so worked up.

But I have to say that where I was concerned he was caution itself. He never took risks with me. He always watched over me.

I was scared standing by that big, hard expanse of road. It seemed so far to cross. In fact I couldn't even see the land on the other side because the road sloped up to the middle and then dropped down out of sight.

'What's over there?' I whimpered.

'Just like here, rough ground . . .' Dog told me. Then his voice got drowned out by a big tanker lorry that thundered past us. The thing towered above us. It was hot and terribly noisy. It also blew out foul smoking air that made me gasp and choke. The wheels were taller than a table in the table place. They spun round and kicked up the surface of the road so that we were sprayed with grit and small stones.

I ran back to the shelter of some stunted, dusty bushes. I was shaking so much I almost couldn't stand.

'Let's go back to our nest,' I pleaded with Dog when he came to get me.

But he had that determined look that I was beginning to recognize.

'We can't, Little. You know we can't.'

'Please, Dog,' I begged.

'Go back – and then what?' he barked.

'We'll find another way to get water,' I argued.

'There is no other way . . .'

One of those big bus things that carry numbers of humans roared past. Then a car raced past, overtaking the bus. Then another car came from the other direction and made a terrible *blaring* noise at the car that was overtaking.

'I'll never get across there, Dog!' I whimpered. 'I'm too terrified even to try.'

'I'll be with you,' he whispered in my ear.

'So we'll both be killed together!' I protested. 'What's the sense of that?'

He put his head on one side and looked at me solemnly. 'I certainly wouldn't want to be alive without you,' he said. 'Not now. I've grown used to having you here!'

Then he grinned and I saw the tip of his lovely long tongue peeping out of the corner of his mouth and I loved him so much I thought: Oh! Let's get it over with!

He could sort of read my mind and he knew I was ready.

'We go to the side of the road. I will be standing beside you. Whatever is coming on the road won't touch you. Not while you're on the side. So stand firm! No running away! Promise?'

I think I nodded. I can't be certain. I was finding it very hard to move at all.

'Then,' he continued, 'when I think the time is right – and you have to trust me and not go running off on your own . . . Are you listening?'

'Yes! Yes, I'm listening. Only do it soon, Dog, or I'll flop down here and never move again.'

'When I think the time is right I'll bark "Now". As soon as you hear that, run straight for the other side as fast as you can.'

Well! It *sounded* all right. But I suspected that *doing* it would be quite a different matter.

'NOW!' he barked and I saw him skittering across the road as fast as a rat. It was only when he'd disappeared over on the other side that I realized I hadn't moved a step. He'd barked 'Now' and I'd remained stuck to the ground.

Now . . . we were apart. We were separated by that dreadful road. This was worse than anything. Now he was there and I was here. I'd have to go on living – this side of the road – without him . . . for ever. I could feel my tail pressing down behind my rear legs. I could feel a terrible lump of pain and panic in my throat. I thought then that I'd rather die in the middle of the road than go on living on this side of it without him.

A huge petrol tanker bellowed in front of me, spewing black fumes and leaving the air all crinkled in its wake.

Then through this jangled, shattered light I thought I saw Dog again. He was racing towards me over the surface of the nightmare road. I saw – yet didn't see! The air was so thick with petrol fumes and heat that I thought I was having a vision or a dream.

A moment later and there he was, skidding to a halt beside me and swinging round to face me at the same time.

'What happened?' he gasped. He was breathing so fast that he could scarcely speak. 'You didn't come!' he panted. He sounded quite cross.

'I'm sorry!' I whimpered.

Looking back I'm quite ashamed of how I behaved. I'm much braver now. But then I was still very timid and, of course, I couldn't possibly know all the much greater dangers that were waiting for us and that we'd have to survive before we found the magic garden. And even after that; even after meeting Joanna and David, even then life had some cruel tricks to play on us.

'Listen to me, Little,' Dog said. 'I'm going to say "Now" and when I do I shall stay right here until I see you move. I shall bite you if I have to. And if you don't run straight across that road then I shall be run over. Me! Not you! Because I shall be running *behind* you and I shall be in much greater danger. So if you care about me . . . you'll *run*. Is that quite clear?'

I managed to nod.

He went behind me, just like he said he would. I could even feel his hot breath fanning the fine hairs on the plume of my tail.

'Look straight ahead,' he growled, forcing me to face the horrible road.

A motorbike tore past, then a van came in the other direction. Two cars, driving quite slowly, followed by a long caravan. Another motorbike. A lorry. A lorry passing the lorry. Smoke and fumes and grit and flying stones. Heat bouncing off the surface and petrol leaking from machines. Tar and filth. An empty cigarette packet, thrown out of a window. Wheels turning, spokes spinning. Noise blaring; zooming and booming and grinding and—

'NOW, Little!' Dog yelled in my ear and I felt his teeth pinch my rump.

'Ow!' I shrieked and I shot straight across the road, with my eyes fixed on the other side.

A lorry honked its horn and I heard the sound of brakes screeching.

I rolled over and over on the coarse, gritty surface and slithered down a slight decline into a gutter of rubbish and old tin cans. I realized my eyes were shut. I didn't know how I was going to open them ever again. I felt with a paw to see if Dog was beside me. But I could feel only dirt and stones and horrible piles of human mess.

'DOG!' I yelped. My eyes snapped open and I leaped to my feet. 'Oh, Dog! Where are you?' I choked. I turned in a circle, my eyes blurred with tears, my heart pounding. 'Dog!' I sobbed again.

'I'm here, Little!' I heard him whisper and he put his head on my shoulder and licked my face.

Chapter Six

Well! Now we were there: 'The Other Side of the Road'. It was as if we were visiting a foreign country and had just passed the frontier. Far behind us, across that terrible divide, was all that was familiar and safe and everything that I'd ever experienced in my life. Ahead lay the unknown.

'You told me you wanted an adventure,' Dog growled.

'I never did,' I protested.

'Yes, you did.'

'When? When did I say anything so stupid?'

'The night we met.'

'I don't recall it.'

'Well, I do.'

'If I did say anything as . . . stupid as that – and I'm not saying that I did – then, obviously, I meant an adventure like . . . like . . . like running out into the big water until you can feel your feet leaving the ground and you're running on nothing. Or darting into the table place and jumping onto a chair and grabbing food off a plate before the human comes to clear it away. I didn't mean . . . risking our lives and ending up as strangers in an alien land . . .'

I was in a really mean mood. I expect it was my nerves that were to blame, caused by the shock of crossing the road.

But, honestly! The place we'd arrived at was far worse than anything I could have imagined.

We were walking up a rough, dirt road. We couldn't even see the distant hills from where we were, nor the big water. All around us were long walls of drab grey material. I can't even begin to describe this stuff, but I know I must try. It was as if morning mist had been gathered together and then somehow made solid. Through these walls – exactly like looking through mist – you could dimly see what lay on the other side. The walls enclosed huge rooms – endlessly long and wide – crammed with a jungle of dark green plants, dripping in a murky half light.

When a breeze was blowing, the walls moved. They sort of sighed and shuddered – like Mother used to when she was asleep and we pups were huddled up against her for warmth. Once in a while we would find a place where the stuff had come loose from the frame that supported it. It made a strange, rattling, flapping sound and it waved in the breeze, like human washing on a line. The stuff had a horrid non-smell; I mean, it did smell – quite strongly, really – but it smelled of nothing that has ever been alive. I didn't like it at all.

'What is it?' I whispered to Dog.

'Humans make it,' he replied.

'What for?'

'These things,' he said, sounding irritated. He got like that when I asked him something to which he didn't really know the answer.

I stared at the great, grey, see-through wall.

'They *make* it?' I repeated, with a kind of disbelief.

'I heard two humans talking about it once . . .'

That's how he got most of his information, I was beginning to realize – listening to humans talking. Dog was a great listener. But I sometimes wondered if what he heard could be taken for the truth. I've listened to humans talking – we dogs do. Of course we do; we have to. But very often what they are saying is such drivel that I get bored and go away. I once heard two humans discussing what they were going to eat. They went on for hours – just discussing what they were going to eat. I ask you! We dogs eat what we find. If we discussed it first and then tried to find what we'd discussed . . . well! The dog race would have died out years ago.

But Dog, my Dog, he listened and listened and really it didn't always make him any the wiser. (He was wisest when he used his own dog-sense. Then he was wise indeed.)

But now he was insisting on telling me what the humans had said about the horrible, grey, un-living stuff that never goes away.

'They said it was called "plastic" – something like that.' I've also noticed that humans give a name to every blessed thing. 'Plastic'! What sort of a name was that? 'They said,' Dog continued, 'that the only way it could ever be destroyed was by burning it and that even then it never completely went away. Humans are very clever . . .'

'Or very foolish!' I rejoined. I could see no point at all in making something that never went away. I might not, at that time, have lived for very long but I had seen the spring flowers blossom, nod in the air, and then gradually die. I had seen the seed heads that formed and Dog himself had told me how the seed heads made new flowers. I'd seen the big water throw tiny shells onto the sand and how the shells had been ground down until they became sand and how sometimes the sand had disappeared and there was rock and pebble in its place.

I'd seen my sister, the unlucky one, die.

I'd seen the bare twigs of trees grow green with leaf and I'd seen the leaf turn brown in the sun. I'd seen birds with pointed tails skim in low over the ground and take up residence under the roofs of human houses. I didn't know where they came from, but I'd seen them come; and I wasn't so dumb that I couldn't work out that if they came from somewhere, then one day they'd probably go back there. Like we, one day, would go back to the big water (I hoped and prayed).

'I think,' I said, 'that everything that lives comes and goes.' I felt quite indignant about it. 'I think it very foolish to try to make something that stays for ever.'

Dog looked at me and grinned then. 'You're a big thinker!' he said.

But I'm not; not really. Not like he was. I just, sometimes, see how stupid humans can be. Some humans. At that point in my life I hadn't met any good ones. At that point, I thought humans were creatures to be avoided at all costs. It was going to be quite a while before we started to meet good humans. But when we did we met very good ones indeed.

That's why I wanted to tell this story, really. To sort of celebrate the good humans – who made up for all the bad ones. And by the end you will discover that I know a lot of good humans. In the magic garden they are all good – though some are better than others. And most of them can still talk such a lot of drivel.

That night Dog and I slept behind a pile of empty wooden boxes. Or I should say rather that we tried to sleep. It wasn't easy because we discovered that the Plastic Place – as we called it – was overrun by armies of rats. Now a rat I can cope with. But an army of rats is altogether different. An army of rats could easily attack us and I don't think we would have stood much of a chance against them. Their numbers would have overwhelmed us. Luckily for us they were busy stealing from the plastic houses. They got away with quantities of tomatoes. I don't like tomatoes. So we went to bed hungry, tired – and thirsty.

'Where's all the water you promised?' I whispered to Dog.

'Tomorrow,' he growled. He was lying with his head on the ground between his paws and his eyes were open. 'You go to sleep, Little,' he whispered. 'I'll keep guard.'

Chapter Seven

We didn't stay for many nights behind the boxes. It wasn't much of a place and the rats had got the scent of us. They didn't actually attack us but they did run very close on a number of occasions. Each time Dog stood his ground and barked at them, which frightened them off. But you have to go carefully with rats, they're much more intelligent than one supposes them to be. They can work things out if they're in a group. One rat is quite stupid, really. But a number of rats together seem to get extra intelligence. I thought them quite scary and even Dog was more jumpy and nervous than usual.

'We'll have to go, Little,' he said one night when a group of about ten of them had all run at our nest and had stood staring, with their tails flicking, taking not a scrap of notice of Dog's barking.

The thing that finally scared them off was a human coming along with a big mangy dog which he kept on a length of rope. The man was carrying a light. He shone it into all the dark corners and the dog snuffled and whined incessantly. The rats scattered as soon as they got scent of him and Dog ducked back behind the boxes where I was hiding.

Luckily the human's dog got the scent of the rats first;

the human released it from the rope and it chased off, ignoring the boxes where we were cowering. (Well, I was. I expect Dog was being more brave.) But:

'It'll come back,' Dog whispered. 'Then it'll get our scent. It's best if we go.'

'But then it'll follow us,' I wailed.

'We'll put him off. Don't worry, I know what to do. Come on, Little. Time to be going.'

And that's what we did, there and then. We just got up and went.

It was a dark night and very warm. There was a bit of breeze blowing up above, but it didn't seem to reach us, surrounded as we were on all sides by the plastic houses. We hurried up a narrow path, ducking and darting from shadow to shadow. Behind us I could hear the human's dog yelping and screeching.

'Sounds like a kill,' Dog said grimly.

'Oh, dear!' I gasped. But actually that was good for us. If the dog had killed a rat it would keep it occupied and give us more of a chance to get away.

But then, just when I was daring to hope that we'd succeeded, a light gleamed up ahead of us and the next moment we saw the man, coming from a side track round the corner of a plastic house and heading straight for us.

'In there, Little!' Dog hissed and he swerved his body, pushing me sideways through a narrow tear in the plastic into the dark, steamy interior of one of the houses.

We had been inside these houses before and always at night. So it wasn't an entirely new experience for me. But this time I was so scared that my heart was pounding and I was sure that the sound of it would give us away even if the human's dog didn't find our scent first.

The air was very hot and moist – like it is sometimes before a storm. Thunder is one of my greatest fears. And lightning is even more frightening. So the stormy atmosphere only added to my panic. I think Dog was really as scared as me, though of course he tried not to show it. He once told me that he had to be brave for both of us and that that made it easier for him. But I think he only said that to cheer me up and to stop me feeling guilty. Because I do feel guilty, even now sometimes, that I left so much up to him. He would tell me what to do – and I just followed. Sometimes he'd even tell me how to feel. 'Don't be frightened, Little,' he'd say – as if saying it would stop me.

And in a way it did. I so wanted to live up to him; to make him proud of me.

Well, that night was the start of our real journey. (Crossing the road was only a taste of what was to come – though, mercifully, we didn't know that at the time.)

That night the human's dog *did* get our scent and the next thing we knew was a terrifying barking and shouting and the light flashing outside the plastic house. Then, suddenly, the dog was *inside*. It must have squeezed through the same gap that we had used. Once the dog was inside it started running like a whirlwind, here and there, barking and growling and snapping and yelping.

The plants in this particular house were all long and thin and grew up sticks. There were bright red tomatoes hanging on them.

The human's dog was making a terrible mess. Tomatoes were bouncing off the stalks and the plants were being knocked here and there. But, much worse, it was making straight for us. Its nose was firmly on the ground and we could hear the sniffing it made from the other side of the house.

28

'He's got us!' Dog whispered. 'Come on, Little!'

I didn't need any encouragement. I followed Dog so closely that my nose was practically up his bottom.

We ran up one path through the plants and then doubled back down another. Dog seemed to be looking for something. I couldn't imagine what it was. All I wanted was to get out of the plastic house as fast as possible and run far away. But Dog had other plans. (He always had plans.)

'Ah!' he hissed and I saw him squeeze into a narrow, tube-like pipe. I followed at once. It was a really tight fit. Dog was ahead and he couldn't turn round, so once again I had my nose squashed against his rump. I didn't like the feeling at all. It was like being shut into a small space, with hardly any air. It was even hotter, because of the heat of our bodies, and I began to think that I'd suffocate if we didn't get out soon.

'What is this place?' I yelled.

'Keep your voice down,' he hissed. 'I think the humans wind the plastic round these tubes. I saw one yesterday, near the boxes.'

'But are we safe here?'

'Yes,' Dog whispered.

'Why?' I didn't want to doubt him but I couldn't see what made him so certain.

'Because we're little, Little.'

And so I learned another lesson. Big dogs can't get into small spaces. It can be quite useful being little.

Meanwhile, outside the pipe-thing in the plastic house the human's dog was getting thrashed for all the mess it had made. The human was really livid and was whipping it — with the rope, I suppose.

I couldn't bear to hear the dog yelping and the sound of the rope on its thin flesh. I know the dog was out to get us; I know it was our enemy. But I hated the sound of it being punished. The whining and the vile, shouting voice of the human.

Poor dogs that live with cruel masters. They can't help but be cruel themselves.

We didn't leave the pipe-thing until the first light was glimmering in the sky and the birds were waking up. When we did finally emerge we had to stretch quite a lot before we could even move properly — we'd been cramped for so long. Then Dog found water squirting out of a hole. We both drank a lot of it and got soaked at the same time. I didn't mind. I liked it. It cooled me down. We went out and found some human food, thrown away in a corner near some paper and old tins. Humans throw away more food than they eat, I sometimes think. They are very wasteful — but then that can be quite useful to us other animals.

I saw Dog looking round, with a worried expression. I was beginning to recognize those expressions. I could almost tell precisely what Dog was thinking — well, what he was feeling would be more correct — by the look on his face. The worried expression usually ended in trouble.

'This place is no good for us, Little,' he said. 'We must try to get to the high ground, away from these humans.'

'Why?' I asked. 'Humans are useful.'

'Yes — but this isn't safe for us. The humans won't want us here. We'll always be on guard. We need somewhere where humans don't bother us, where they hardly notice we exist. Somewhere more . . . peaceful.' He had a strange look in his eyes as he spoke.

'Peaceful?' I said in a small voice. 'Where?' My heart was beating too fast again. Panic, I suppose.

'You remember how we used to see the hills from the beach?' he said. 'And the high, white mountains beyond? We should go there.'

'How?' I gasped. It seemed such a long, long way. I'd never been more than a day's walk in my entire life.

'We'll find a way,' he promised me. And right there and then we started off on the next stage of our journey.

Chapter Eight

It took us two days to get clear of the plastic place. The further up the valley we went, the fewer vegetable houses we would pass. Then, just when we'd think we were finally free of them, they would crop up again — scattered about in an untidy, unplanned way.

The first night we had to sleep in the open; curled up in a clump of tall, spiky grasses. Of course, we always had slept in the open, but usually we found somewhere to make ourselves a bit of a nest — a bush, or an angle of wall, or behind boxes like our previous home.

Home! The only home that I'd really known had been the human's yard with Mother and the rest of the family. But when I thought of home I actually remembered the place under the sweet-smelling bush, near the water channel — the nest that Dog and I had first shared. I soon discovered it was wisest not to mention this to Dog. It only made him angry. For ages I didn't know why, but then I realized that he was feeling guilty; guilty for having dragged us away in the first place.

'Maybe we could have managed,' he once said.

'Managed what?' I asked.

'Without water,' he'd replied.

Of course we couldn't. We both knew that. Without water, you die. And he'd been right about the plastic place. There was plenty of water there; the humans used it all the time, to make the vegetables grow.

'But what do they do with them all?' I asked Dog that night, as we were trying to sleep in the clump of grasses.

'They send them away in the big lorries.'

'What for?'

'Go to sleep, Little.'

Then, later, I said: 'But where do the big lorries go?'

There was a pause, then I heard him growl: 'Sleep, Little!'

'But . . .' I persisted and my voice must have sounded a bit whiny – it can sometimes, I know – because he suddenly turned on me and growled, really fiercely.

I was so surprised that I shot out of the grass and ran away from him. Then I ducked into the long grass further up the track and lay there trembling.

'Little,' I heard him call after a moment. 'Little, come back.'

But I stayed hidden. I was really shocked by his reaction. He'd never growled at me like that before.

'Little,' he called again. 'Come on. Come back.'

But I still stayed where I was. I didn't trust him, growling like that. Why was he angry with me? What had I done? No, I thought, I'm not going to go back to him until he's said he's sorry. For a long time nothing happened and I began to think he might have gone away. I must admit that made me feel nervous but then, just as I was about to raise my head from my hiding place to see where he was, I heard him call again.

'Little!' His voice sounded so sad. He's unhappy, I thought. I'm making him unhappy because I ran away from him. I couldn't bear that.

He was sitting on his rump on the mud track. When I came near enough to make out his form through the thin, moonlit dark I saw that his head was lowered and his body was shaking.

He looks like a little pup, I thought. A lost and frightened little pup. I ran to him then and licked his cheek and showed him that I loved him really.

'I don't know where the lorries go,' he whispered. 'I don't know what the humans do with all the vegetables. I don't know half the things you ask me.'

'That's all right,' I comforted him. 'Most of the things, we don't really need to know anyway. I always did ask too much.'

He slept that night and I lay beside him listening to his deep breathing. I was thinking about how sad he'd been when he thought he'd lost me and how important he thought it was to answer all my questions. I squeezed myself closer to him and lay with my head and one leg across his slowly breathing body. Whatever happens in the future, I thought, so long as Dog is beside me it won't be too bad.

Towards evening on the following day we came to a place where there was a house.

'Humans!' Dog said, sniffing the air. 'Human food!' he added.

The thought made my heart sing. We'd been subsisting on a diet of scraps and raw meat: mice, mainly, and once or twice I'd caught a bird for us. I was quite good at catching birds. I still am. I'm good at catching them; I don't at all mind killing them. But I'm not so keen on eating them. I don't like all the feathers. They make me cough.

Human food is altogether different; the food they give to dogs, I mean. It's nearly always chopped up and often it's cooked. Cooked food is . . . all right; though I don't think it's got much goodness left in it. And very often the scraps that are left raw are the bits that I'd leave myself if I'd had enough to eat. No! The best thing about human food is that it comes ready and delivered. I mean, you don't have to chase about trying to catch it. You don't have to hunt and pounce and very often miss your prey. Human food – if they know you're there and want to give it to you – comes at a regular time each day. That makes everything much more simple and relaxed. Even when they don't know you're there, they still leave stuff lying about which is quite easy to steal if you're quick and use your brain. (Don't steal while the human is about. They always go off somewhere in the end.)

The best possible thing for a dog is to keep a human or two about the place. They think about food most of the time and eat sometimes as much as three times a day. They are therefore the source of unlimited supplies.

The house we'd now found, however, didn't look entirely promising. It was small and not very clean. Human places usually smell of soap and stuff they put in water to wash the floor. It's a smell I like. I like clean places. When Dog and I had the nest by the water channel we never made our mess near it. We always went away to do that. We did eat food in it sometimes. But dogs eat up everything; every scrap, not a crumb is left. In fact that's one of the ways we clean the nest. We eat everything that we find lying in it. But this place smelled of dirt. Real, smelly human dirt.

'I don't like it,' I said wrinkling up my nose. But we went towards it anyway.

'Best if we at least find out,' Dog advised.

It was well after noon. The sun was high in the sky. We were both tired and hungry — we were always hungry in those days.

'Go on then,' I told him — making him go first. I told myself it was because he was better at it than I was — checking places, I mean. But I really think I'm a coward at heart. I get easily scared. Dog was much braver. I hope I told him that at the time. I'm sure I must have.

So I hung back a little and followed more slowly as he dodged his way towards the house, going from clump to clump of grass and sometimes crawling on his stomach across open ground. I don't know where he learned all his tricks. He certainly knew how to get by.

Dog was nearly at the half-open door of the house when I heard a funny, metal *click!* I felt sure that he must have heard it as well. But I noticed that he was still going forward. Maybe the noise his body was making on the rough ground prevented him hearing the sound. It was a human sound, I was sure of that. And I don't know why, but it made me instantly nervous.

So much so that I shot up, breaking my cover, and shouted out his name. 'Dog!' I barked.

I saw Dog look back over his shoulder, surprised.

At the same moment the door of the house swung open and a fat human appeared. It was a man and he had a long, shining metal stick held in his hands. He was pointing the stick straight at Dog.

Everything was happening very quickly and yet it seemed strangely slow at the same time. I saw the man. I saw the stick. I saw Dog looking round at me, over his shoulder. I saw all the burned grass on the ground and a fly on a stone. I even noticed a little cloud in the sky and a spider in its web.

It was as if I saw everything there was to see in the world all in that instant.

And then the next moment there was a shattering *bang!* and I saw the end of the metal stick explode into sudden flame and smoke and a stone near Dog jumped as if someone had kicked it.

The man broke his stick in half. Then he mended it again, very quickly. He pointed it once more at Dog.

'Run, Dog! Run!' I screamed and as I did so, I turned my back and sped away across the dried-up, thorny earth. A moment later I heard another terrifying *bang!* This only made me run faster and further. I knew I had to get away from that man.

I was charging through tall grasses and thistles and thorn bushes. I didn't let anything stop me. In my panic I didn't notice how torn and bruised my body was becoming. I didn't even feel the pain. I only knew that I must get far away from the man with the exploding stick.

Eventually I came to a place where winter water runs. I recognized it as similar to the river that in winter came running and gushing and bubbling – pushing down through the stones onto the beach before it met, and then disappeared into, the big water. Now, of course, this river was almost dry. But there were still some long, stagnant puddles. I turned there and splashed my way up one of them. It was good to feel the water spraying onto my body and cooling my feet. When I reached the end it was only a short distance across parched rock before I came to another, even longer channel. The water wasn't so deep that my feet left the ground. I just splashed and waded through it. I continued in this way for quite some time before eventually I came to where the stones took over completely and the water disappeared.

Now the going became more difficult. The land had been rising steadily all the way and sometimes I had to climb up steep little cliffs. But at least there were no thorn bushes to tear at me. So I continued to run and scramble and slip and slide up the parched, rocky river centre between its low, grassy banks.

Finally, gasping for breath and weak from running under the terrible heat of the sun, I collapsed in the shade of some dusty trees. There was a pool of brown, sour water there and I drank and drank, choking and gasping at the same time. I was so hot that I put my entire head into the pool. The water got into my nose and made me sneeze violently. I crawled back into the shade and lay panting.

Then I waited for Dog to arrive.

Perhaps I slept a little. I'm not sure. I only remember that suddenly the air was cooler as the sun was losing its strength. I stood up and went down to the puddle of water. I drank a little of it. It tasted foul. But at least it was wet. Then I looked round, listening and sniffing.

'Dog!' I barked. The sound seemed to echo on the still air. 'Dog!'

No answer came back. I scratched the back of my neck and wondered what to do. Behind the trees, the ground rose steeply for a short way. I scrambled up to the top of this hill.

The valley lay stretched in front of me with the plastic place gleaming like a strange lake far below. There was land in every direction as far as the eye could see and where the land ended, far, far away on the horizon I thought I saw the faint blue smudge of the big water.

'Dog!' I called. 'Dog!'

A few birds rose, twittering from the land and somewhere

miles away a dog was barking. But it wasn't my dog; it wasn't Dog.

'Dog!' I called again. But this time there was only silence.

I knew then that I'd lost him and that in doing so I'd also lost myself. I returned to the trees near the puddle and dug myself a shallow nest. Then I curled up and whined myself into a fitful, uneasy sleep.

I dreamed that night that I was seeing him sitting trembling like a young pup; the way he had been when I'd run away from him only the night before. Was he trembling now? I wondered, waking with a start. Was he alone and miserable like I was? Or had the man with the exploding stick hurt him? Was he lying somewhere out in that great mass of land that I'd seen, wounded and unable to move?

The night was dark and the breeze was quite chilly. It sighed in the trees; a strange, sad sound.

'Oh, Dog!' I sobbed and I whimpered myself back to sleep again.

Chapter Nine

The next day I didn't feel very well. I think now, looking back, that it might have been the water I'd drunk from the puddle that was making me feel sick. I was very hot inside my head as well. I felt as I did when I had the fish bone stuck in my mouth. The memory of that time made me instantly sad and lonely. I desperately wanted Dog there to look after me and help me to feel better.

As the day progressed my fever grew worse. Although I was hungry, I couldn't be bothered to go and find food. I just lay in my shallow nest beneath the dusty trees and waited for Dog to find me.

I was sure he would come soon. He had a brilliant sense of smell. When we used to play on the beach I could never hide from him. He always knew exactly where I was because he followed the trail of my scent.

Now all he would have to do was follow that scent for a longer time. I decided it was only the distance that was delaying him. If I trusted him and waited, he would be bound to find me eventually.

Meanwhile the sun moved slowly across a startlingly blue sky. High summer was upon us and the heat was becoming more intense every day.

When we lived on the beach, humans used to come during the summer months and lie stretched out with their pink skins glistening and sweating until they went red and sore. They haven't even fur to protect them as we have and they usually wear things called clothes. But on the beach they'd have practically nothing covering them and they'd let the sun beat down on them. Then they'd run into the big water and splash about – I suppose to cool themselves. Then back they'd go to their place on the sand and cover their bodies with stuff from a bottle. (It smelled rather sweet, like flowery oil. I quite liked it.) After that, they'd lie back and let the sun scorch down on them again until they burned like bread under a flame. I really think humans are the most peculiar animals of all. We dogs like a little sun, of course we do. The spring sun is young and exciting to feel. The autumn sun is old and gentle. But the summer sun? That's the sun that kills. Humans don't know much, for all their talk and lorries and plastic places.

When the sun was setting that day I realized that I hadn't eaten anything. I'd scarcely moved. I'd crawled down to the puddle a few times. The water there was getting more and more thick and disgusting, but it was all there was to quench my thirst. On another occasion I'd left the nest to make mess. I noticed that my body felt weak when I tried to walk and the heat that was raging inside me was nearly as fierce as the sun's rays.

A whole day has passed, I thought, and Dog still hasn't found me.

I had a sleepless night but at least I was able to enjoy the cooler air. Not many animals came near my nest. Once a fox passed by and sniffed at me out of curiosity and soon after dawn a partridge landed near the puddle and took a swift drink. I should have tried to catch it for food, but I was too weary.

The following day I was weaker.

If I stay here I shall die, as sister died, I thought. But I was determined that I wouldn't 'lose the will to live', so instead I forced myself to move.

I waited until evening, when the sun was less strong. I knew that first I should find cleaner water and after that I'd have to get myself some food. The only other water I could think of was back down the river – the way I'd come. There were the two channels that I'd run through when escaping from the man with the exploding stick. That water would surely be fresher than in my fast dwindling puddle. It was deeper there – and I was sure that deeper water would remain pure longer. So I decided to retrace my steps. Another good point about this plan was that I'd be going in the direction that Dog was bound to come looking for me. I quite cheered up at the thought of meeting him along the way.

It wasn't a comfortable journey. Not only was I much weaker than I'd thought, but the little cliffs had been easier to climb up than they were to descend. I kept slipping and falling and the rock was hard and jagged where I landed. By the end of the night I'd gone a depressingly short distance and when the sun came up I was in a bleak, barren area of low rocks and parched, dusty earth. There were no trees there to give me shade and the bushes were sparse of leaf and horribly thorny.

I was now feeling terribly depressed and the fever was raging through my body. I felt unable to take another step and lay down amongst a jumble of small rocks and pebbles in the full blaze of the sun.

I must have drifted off to sleep. Later I woke with a sudden start. I could hear birds squawking noisily. I searched the dazzling sky through half closed eyes, looking for them. But the light hurt my eyes, so I turned over on my side and gradually focused again. I saw the birds at once. They were flying in and around a clump of trees slightly up the side of the valley at some considerable distance from me. The trees looked green and lush. I could just imagine the cool shade that they would offer. I decided to abandon the river. Shade seemed even more attractive than water to me, as the sun beat down.

But, oh! it was a long journey. I had to go uphill and the thorns and stones and dust were there every step of the way. More than once I wondered if I was doing the right thing. Dog might miss my scent. There would be no water. I might never reach the trees. And the sun was merciless. It cut through my fur, like a knife. I imagined all my flesh opening up and my blood seeping away.

The birds were still squawking. I really believed they were laughing at me. I wondered why they were being so mean to me. What had I ever done to them that they should lead me astray now? Maybe I'd run and caught one of their brothers or sisters and they'd never forgiven me. Maybe the birds were having their revenge for all the times I had chased them.

But, in fact, those birds were my saviours. Because when I did finally reach the trees I discovered that they were growing in a hollow and that the grass there was green and lush and there were even a few pink and blue flowers still in bloom. But it was the sound that most gladdened my heart. If anyone were to ask me what is the most beautiful sound I've ever heard, I would have to say it was the dripping, splashing sound of running water that I heard that day. I felt refreshed by that sound even before I found the source of it; and when I found the source of it I could honestly have yelped with joy.

Humans had made a square, stone basin. They'd fitted it into the side of the hill. The flowers and grass grew thickly round it. Even the trees seemed to lean over as if they were reaching down towards it with open pleasure. Into this basin, out of the side of the hill, water dripped and gurgled and flowed. So much water that the basin was full. There was a pipe from it that took away the overflow. I suppose humans used it, somewhere further down the valley.

I lay on the side of that hill in a sort of waking dream. The grass was cool and sweetly scented. The birds that had seemed to be laughing at me were now trilling and singing. The air was soft and moist; the shade, exquisite. After revelling in this bliss for a while I crawled, pulling my aching body forward, until my head was over the side of the basin. Finally, taking my time to appreciate every moment, I started to lap at the surface of the water with my parched tongue.

It was the most perfect sensation of my entire life. The water was new and cold. It sent a tingle of ice through every nerve of my body. It was pure and clean. It tasted of fresh air and early morning sunlight.

I drank until I could drink no more. Then I felt suddenly sick. I scrambled back from the basin and ran away into the undergrowth. I didn't want to foul this beautiful place. I think I knew at once that it was going to be my home.

I was really very sick. I expect I'd drunk the water too fast. But even being sick seemed to be good for me. It cleared the foul puddle water out of my body. When I'd finished I was able to go back to the basin and taste the clean spring water in my mouth again.

At last, completely refreshed, I rolled over in the soft, cool grass and went to sleep.

Chapter Ten

I don't remember how long I stayed in the glade by the water. The days passed without my counting them.

At first I felt safe and almost happy there; having water and shade made all the difference. Of course I knew that the water would have to be shared. Pure, flowing water is the greatest luxury during the long summer days and the basin would be bound to attract a lot of creatures.

It was mainly the foxes that came. They would appear with such stealth that I never heard them until they were almost beside me. We left each other alone, the foxes and I. I once saw a dog in a fight with one. It happened in amongst some bushes down near the big water and I suspect the dog had started it. But the fox put up a good fight. It badly wounded the dog, and in the end, when it got away it didn't seem to have suffered the slightest injury itself. I learned then that a fox can be a quick, vicious fighter and I've been wary of them ever since. They also have a strange, strong smell. In fact I could always tell when a fox had arrived by its smell long before I actually saw it.

Sometimes other dogs would come to the water basin and there were always the birds. I think they lived in the trees that surrounded the glade and I decided not to chase them because I thought they lived too near to me and that they could all gang up on me if I provoked them. I've never seen birds attacking a dog, but Dog told me that he'd once seen a giant bird drop down out of the sky and pick up a cat and carry it off. I expect that was just one of his stories but you can't be too careful when you're living on your own in the wild.

The dogs didn't bother me — although some of them were a bit over-curious and once or twice I had to snap and snarl. If I got the chance I would ask if any of them had seen Dog. I'd tell them that he was about my height. That his fur was black with white markings. That he had a kind face and the sort of ears that stick up from the head. But not one of them seemed to recognize him from my description.

Each day I would go further and further from the glade, back towards the river, looking for Dog. I'd climb up to a high point and bark his name. But I never got any answer. I began to fear that maybe the man with the stick had hurt him badly. The stick was obviously used for something and I kept remembering how the first time I'd heard it bang, a stone had jumped up out of the ground as if it'd been kicked. These two events — the bang and the stone jumping — seemed somehow connected, though I couldn't see how.

So each day I looked for him and each evening I came back disappointed. Nor was I having a lot of luck with hunting. I caught a few small birds and once or twice a mouse or young rat. Sometimes on my travels I'd come across fruit lying on the ground under stunted, little trees and I ate a lot of yellow corn that grows on tall frond-like plants and is covered with a thick leaf and masses of fine hair. The hair stuck in my throat and the corn, when I got to it, was hard and unripe and bitter. But it filled up my stomach and made me feel fed, even if, as I suspected, I was beginning to starve from lack of nourishing food. I was certainly becoming very thin and each day I noticed my movements getting weaker.

One day I was resting near the basin when a big, wolf-like dog came there to drink. I was wary at first. It looked such a fierce creature. But after coming and sniffing me, it padded away and just stared at me from the other side of the basin. It stayed in the glade all that hot afternoon and after a while we started to get quite friendly. I've often noticed that big dogs are more friendly towards me. I don't know why. Maybe they think I'm like a young pup and they want to protect me. Anyway I asked this wolf dog if he'd seen Dog on his travels and I told him about the man and the stick. He knew all about these things. He said the stick is called a 'gun' and that humans use them to kill animals and birds. He said he lived with a human and that they'd often go out together and the human would bang the gun and, when he did, the wolf dog had to bring back the dead birds and animals that he'd killed and give them to him. I suppose really it's no different to us when we go hunting. Only the humans use a machine to do the work for them. But then humans always use machines to save them having to do things themselves. I asked the wolf dog if his human would bang at a dog. He said banging was called 'shooting' and that some humans do shoot dogs if they're taking their crops or their chickens.

The night after we'd had this conversation and I was alone in the glade I couldn't stop thinking about Dog. The wolf dog's stories disturbed me. What if the man had killed Dog? What if his body was lying near the human's house and only I would know who he was or care that he was dead.

The following morning I knew I'd have to go back. I'd have to look for Dog, even if it was only his dead body that I found. I had to know whether he had escaped or not. If he had and we'd lost each other then I could live in the hope of one day seeing him again. But what if he was dead? Then, I thought I'd have to cry myself better because that's what he'd want me to do. I'd have to go on living without him. But at least I'd know and I'd always remember him.

When I was leaving the glade that day I stopped and looked back. I had every intention of returning there, but not until I'd found out what had happened to Dog. I realized then that although this was a good place, it had always been empty for me. There was water and there was shade; there was green grass to lie in and the sound of the birds to wake me each morning. There was a bush covered with flowers that smelled sweet in the evening warmth and there was a rocky outcrop from where I could see right down the valley to the big water. It was in every way a perfect spot. But Dog hadn't been there with me. I knew then that I would rather have lived in a dusty yard or behind boxes in the plastic place with Dog beside me than in that beautiful glade without him.

I wasn't even sorry to be going. I couldn't think why it had taken me so long to do so. I was glad the wolf dog had come along and told me about humans and their guns. Now I was setting out to find Dog with a new determination. Of course I was a bit afraid and I wasn't sure that I'd find my way, but it was worth the try.

I turned and ran as fast as I could away down the hill towards the dry river bed and the parched land beyond. I never once again looked back at my water-glade under the trees.

Chapter Eleven

Time, the counting of the passing of the days, had completely escaped me. I had no idea how long it had been since I first left Mother and the others. It seemed like another life. But so did living with Dog in the nest under the sweet-smelling bush. That was when I was at my happiest, though I had some fond memories of our journey through the plastic place as well. Dog could do that: he made the scary exciting, and the downright nasty, bearable.

It was the memory of him that spurred me on. I wanted so much to see him again that it made me brave. Without this braveness nothing would have persuaded me to go back towards the plastic place, searching for the human's house with the dirty smell.

I soon reached the river and turned downhill towards the big water. But, of course, the summer sun had been beating down on it and the water channels had all but dried up. So I wasn't sure where along the river bed I should turn off and start crossing the thorny land.

I suppose I started to get lost right from the start. There was no scent left for me to follow – it had all been too long ago – and the whole valley had such a sameness about it that there weren't familiar landmarks to guide me. Besides,

I'd only done the journey once. I didn't really know the place at all.

Finally, after a whole day wandering under a blistering sun, I reached a hard surfaced road. This wasn't a road like the terror down beside the big water. It was much narrower for one thing and it had hardly any traffic on it. Sometimes a car would pass and once in a while a small truck. But there weren't lorries on it. Not huge ones like I'd seen on the morning we left the beach.

I knew humans used these roads to get from one place to another. So I thought if I ran along beside it, it would at least lead me to somewhere where humans were living. I needed their scraps and their thrown-away food. I was desperately hungry.

But which way to turn? I reckoned that uphill would take me to the mountains and downhill would take me to the big water. Which would Dog have chosen? I wondered. I puzzled about this for quite some time, trying to put myself inside Dog's head. I decided that that was precisely what he would have done himself. He would have tried to imagine what I would do. He would know that I would be looking for him, if I was able to. He would try to think where I would want to find him. He would remember how much I missed our first nest together under the bush, near the water channel . . .

He would look for me there!

I was so thrilled by this idea that I didn't hesitate. I turned and started to run downhill, along the side of the narrow road. I almost barked with excitement, so sure was I that I'd find Dog curled up in our nest beside the big water, waiting for me. I imagined our reunion. I would tell him how much I loved him. I would yelp with relief and he'd wag his tail till it almost fell off. We'd go to the table place for food and then, in the cool of the evening, we'd splash together in the shallows of the big water and return, tired and happy, to our nest under the bush.

It was such a lovely dream. And I wanted so much to believe it.

Running and skipping round a corner of the road, I nearly tripped over the body of an animal. It was a cat. Flies were buzzing round an open wound on its side. I don't like cats. But I felt sorry for it. I suppose a human had run it over. I remembered my brother and how he never came back from the road.

I went a little way from the body and sat down in the dust. I was shaking and I began to whimper. It was the dead cat, I think, that brought me back to reality.

I had no idea where Dog was. And I knew in my heart I'd never get back to the big water to look for him there. Not really. I'd never dare cross that road again for one thing. And supposing I did somehow manage it and found he wasn't there – what then? I'd never be brave enough to cross the road back to this side again. I only ever did it that first time because Dog made me. I'd be stranded by the big water, still not knowing where he was.

The place where I was sitting was on a corner of the road where the ground fell away steeply to one side. Long shadows were filling the valley and there was an evening haze hanging low over the land after the heat of the day. Distantly a bell was ringing – *clang! clang! clang!* – and I could hear a human calling. There must be a living place somewhere near, I thought. I should follow the sounds and find the humans and get something to eat.

But I didn't move. I just sat there, listening to those sounds and seeing the haze deepening towards dark. I must find somewhere safe to sleep, I thought. I must get some rest.

But I didn't move. I remained where I was in the dust at the side of the road. I was whimpering, but even that seemed effortless. 'I'm sorry, Dog,' I sobbed, 'I can't go any further. I don't know where I am or where I should be or how to look after myself any more. I'm frightened. I almost envy that cat. At least the cat doesn't have to worry any more. I'm sorry, Dog!' I sighed. 'I'm so sorry.'

The stillness of evening can be a frightening experience. The day seems to be dying and there is a moment when there is no sound at all. The birds stop singing and even humans pause, probably without knowing it. They stop talking for an instant. There is this same tiny gap between two *clangs* of a bell, amongst all the noises of the distant traffic. It cuts through all the other sounds of the valley. It is a moment of absolute silence.

Then the night sounds take over. The crickets start trilling, as if they have been switched on by some invisible hand. Humans start talking again; the traffic roars; the bell continues to ring.

In that moment of stillness between day and night I think I knew what it is like to lose the will to live. In that moment I wanted to . . . fade away. Just that! In that moment . . . maybe I did – for that briefest of instants – die?

I could see the road curling down the side of the valley and disappearing into the fading light. There was a spot on it, something tiny, moving slowly up towards me. At first I hardly noticed it. It seemed to be there one moment and gone the next.

I just sat there – and waited. I didn't know what it was I was waiting for. Nothing, really. I remained sitting because there was nothing else to do. Any activity seemed pointless.

Now the moving spot was near enough for me to realize that it was some sort of animal. I couldn't make out what it was precisely. Something not very big. A cat, perhaps.

I scratched my shoulder with a rear paw and noticed how thin my back had grown. I could feel the bones sticking out. There was hardly any flesh on me at all. Maybe I was starving to death, there on the side of the road. I didn't really care. I was long past caring.

Now the animal was close enough for me to see that it had dark-coloured fur. It was trotting up the road towards me. Soon we would meet. Then it disappeared from sight as the road veered away behind an outcrop of land.

I should move, I thought. It isn't wise to meet an unknown animal when you're as weak as I am. It might not be friendly, I thought. It might attack me. But still I remained sitting. I didn't care what happened to me, so why should I worry about an unfriendly animal? Besides, there was still a long stretch of road for it to travel before it reached me; I could always run away at the last moment if I felt I had to.

The creature came into view again. It was on the last stretch of road, lower down the sloping hill, running up towards me with its head down. A small black animal, with strong legs and an arching tail.

I remember I thought: No! It isn't a cat. It's a dog.

And then the dog looked up and although we were still at some distance from each other I could almost see its eyes.

And for some reason, I'll never know why, I stood up. It was just a dog, I told myself. Any dog. But I felt a strange

55

shiver, like warmth on a cold day or water in a dry throat, wriggle through my body. This sensation reached as far as my tail. It made me shudder all over. Even my tail was quivering. At the same time my heart started to beat faster, the fur on my body bristled and my ears pricked up.

The dog had white markings on black fur.

It was staring at me and its mouth was slightly open so that I could see the tip of its tongue. As it drew closer, it slowed its steps from a trot to a walk.

I just stood there, with my tail almost wagging. I didn't dare to hope.

The dog's steps grew slower and slower until, while it was still a fair distance from me, it stopped moving altogether.

We just stood there, the two of us, on that narrow, steep road separated by the evening light, surrounded by the oncoming night.

'Little?' the dog whispered.

Chapter Twelve

When the man had shot with the gun for the second time Dog had felt a sharp pain in his shoulder. He was already running for cover and reached some bushes a moment later. He turned his head to lick the spot where it hurt and tasted blood on his tongue.

'I was lucky, Little,' he told me. 'The thing only grazed me. I think it could have killed me.'

I told him then what the wolf dog had explained to me about human guns and shooting.

We were lying together under some bushes. Soon after we met Dog had made a nest for us. Then he'd gone back down the road to where he said there were some human houses. He said I should wait for him. That was an anxious time for me. We'd only just found each other again and he was going off on his own. I pleaded with him not to. But he insisted.

'You need food, Little,' he explained. 'You need food badly.' Apparently there was a bin thing near the human houses and it was full of scraps. He'd only just eaten there himself a little while before we met.

So, reluctantly, I let him go. He seemed to be away for ages. I really did begin to think I'd lost him again. I got so agitated I started to shake and whimper at the thought. But Dog was right. I was in no fit state to have gone with him. Now, when I thought he'd disappeared again, I tried to get up to run down the road to find him. But my legs were so weak that they trembled under my weight and I was forced to lie down once more.

When he eventually came back, he had a big bone sticking out of his mouth. There was still a lot of meat attached to it and he fed me scraps, pulling them off the bone and putting them in my mouth himself. There was a soft centre in the bone as well. This is some of the best food for a dog. It gives us real nourishment. It's easy to eat and it tastes delicious. I had quite a feast, though I couldn't eat an awful lot. Dog said it didn't matter. He said it would be best not to stuff myself while I was so ill and under-nourished. I didn't really believe I was ill until he told me. I just thought I was a bit weary from my journey. But he was right. I had lost my strength, I was bone thin, and most of all I was terribly tired. Sometimes I would doze off to sleep while we were talking.

Dog buried the rest of the bone near our nest so that we'd have food for the following day. Then, with his help, I staggered down the road to where water passed under it, carried in a narrow human channel.

'This is a good place for us,' I told him as I lapped the water.

'It'll do for now,' he said, 'until you're stronger.'

'Then what?' I asked.

'We're going to the mountains, aren't we?' He said it in such a matter-of-fact way. It was as though all those days and days and more days that we had been apart had never happened.

But first I had to get better. So he took me back to the nest he'd dug for us. Oh, the bliss of lying down beside him and feeling his body next to mine! The relief of not being on my own any more! The joy of hearing his voice and smelling him and feeling his tongue licking my face and inside my ears! It was almost too good. I was terrified that I might be dreaming and that I'd wake up and find I was alone under the bush. I would start to tremble at the thought. Then he would move closer to me, putting a leg over my body and holding me.

In the end he started to tell me about what had happened to him. Sometimes while he was talking I'd drop off to sleep, so I didn't hear it all. But the comfort of his voice was the best thing of all that night. Just to know he was there, near me, started to help me to recover my strength. Dog was all the medicine I needed.

After he'd escaped from the man with the gun, he'd quickly picked up my scent and followed me with ease all the way to the dried-up river bed. But then something terrible happened. He lost the scent.

'I searched everywhere for your smell. I couldn't find you, Little. That never happens to me. I thought maybe a human had come and picked you up. There were some human smells about. But that wasn't surprising because they had obviously been working the ground there. And the smells were not very fresh. At least a day old, I reckoned. So it wasn't a very likely explanation. But where else could you have disappeared to?'

I told him how I'd run up the long water channel to cool my body and my feet.

'That explains it,' he said sadly. Apparently, when you pass through water your scent disappears. Something like that.

So when I'd run up the water channel and then crossed the rocks and continued up the second, even longer, channel I was – literally – putting Dog off my scent. I couldn't believe what I was hearing. All those days and days apart because of such a stupid mistake on my part. A dog in the wild has to know so much. Really it was a miracle that we'd ever got back together. I decided then and there that once I was fit, I was *never* going to leave Dog's side again. Wherever he went, I would go. I couldn't stand the pain of losing him again.

He had searched and searched by the river bed. Then, in desperation, he decided to go back to the big water. He thought that would be my most likely move – to go back where everything was familiar. He couldn't imagine me wandering alone in a strange land. Also he reasoned that I'd be able to find my way there. The good thing about the big water is that you can see it from a great distance, so it isn't hard to find if you really have to.

Dog had been all the way to the big water and back, looking for me. He'd crossed the road and waited at the nest. Then, when I didn't show up, he'd crossed the road again and searched all over the plastic place.

He said he was frantic with worry. He'd spent days crossing and recrossing from side to side of the valley, working his way gradually up towards the hills. But wherever he looked there was no sign of me. I think, eventually, he might have found me in the water-glade. And I told him so, because I wanted to reassure him that he'd been doing the right thing searching for me.

'I might have found you, Little,' he replied grimly. 'But would you have been alive?'

'I did try to hunt for food,' I said in a small, apologetic voice.

'I'm not blaming you, Little. It would have been the same for me. In fact, I blame myself. It was my idea to set out on this journey. I thought we could survive in the wild. But there isn't enough food. I know that now. We need to be near humans.'

'So we have to go back?' I asked. 'Back to the beach? But what about the lack of water?'

'Not back, no!' he said firmly. 'I've been, remember. It's no good at all there. Oh, there's plenty of food about. But there's nowhere for us to live safely. No,' he growled, sitting up and looking towards the dark rolling hills, edged by a luminous night sky. 'There are villages higher up. We used to see their lights at night when we were down by the big water. Remember? We must find our way to one of those villages, nearer to the high mountains.'

Always the high mountains. 'Well, maybe in the morning,' I whispered. And I was sound asleep before he'd settled down again beside me.

Chapter Thirteen

We didn't go at once. We stayed in our nest at the side of the road until I was strong enough to walk properly. Dog brought me food each evening and he helped me down to the water channel several times a day. He said it was very important that I should keep drinking and that I should start to get food inside myself. The rest of the time I just lay in the nest, under the shade of the bushes, and let the long sweltering days slip by in a half-dreaming, half-waking state.

Sometimes Dog would go off for a while. I didn't like it when he wasn't there. I was agitated and kept looking for him. I was afraid that he might meet with an accident and not be able to get back to me. I think if that had happened I'd just have gradually sunk into a deep sleep, there beside the road, and never woken up again. I really believed there was no hope of any future without Dog; I certainly wouldn't have wanted to go on living without him.

But I didn't say any of this to Dog. I couldn't expect him to stay by my side the whole time. That wouldn't have done at all. He'd have got bored in no time. Dog really enjoyed going off on adventures and it would have been quite wrong of me to try to prevent him doing what he enjoyed. So I used to wag him off and then worry and fret until I smelled him coming home again.

Not that his expeditions were entirely selfish – far from it! Dog didn't have a selfish bit in him, not where I was concerned. No! He usually went exploring higher up the valley. He was so determined that eventually we would reach the high mountains that he spent the days looking for the safest route.

Then one evening he came back in a state of great excitement. He made me get up and go with him to the water channel. He was thirsty because he'd been running.

'I've been as far as the village, Little,' he told me.

I remembered the lights I'd seen clustered up on the dark hillside when I'd stood on the beach that evening, with my back to the big water.

'It's good, Little! It may be as good as anywhere we're likely to find. It could be just what we're looking for. A place to make our home.'

'You mean we might stop there?' I asked.

I hardly dared believe my ears. I thought he wanted us to go on journeying for ever; never reaching our destination. Of course, he'd let us rest from time to time and, if the winter was bad, we might possibly stay put in one place for several weeks, but always at the back of his mind would be the idea of getting to the high mountains. I thought that was what he planned for us.

'I would like to see the high mountains,' he admitted when I put this to him later, once we were snuggled down in our nest.

'Then you must,' I said with as much conviction as I could find. I'd never been that interested in the high mountains. Not really. That was Dog's dream and I'd just . . . gone along with it, because I wanted to please him. My dream was much more simple: a nice safe home, friendly humans who would throw out scraps, plenty of water and thick over-head shelter. That's all I'd ever wanted, really. Oh – and Dog there beside me, of course. The overhead shelter is very impor-tant. You need protection from the high sun of summer but also from the winter rains. It is very unpleasant being dripped on by cold water. I think this must be why humans build houses. A roof is rather a good idea. But, of course, a thick bush is quite as effective.

'No, Dog,' I heard myself saying, contrary to everything I was feeling, 'we mustn't give up the idea of getting to the mountains. It's what you've always wanted.'

'Yes! But wait till you see the village, Little. I think it might be a good place to make a base.'

Now this was a new idea of his – making a base. So I thought I'd better get it quite clear in my head before I committed us both to it. Because it was me who always made the final decision. Dog had the ideas, but it was left to me to say whether we did them or not. Even leaving the big water had been down to me in the end. Dog wouldn't have gone if I hadn't agreed to it. He would have carried on trying to persuade me. But if I'd absolutely refused, he wouldn't have gone without me. It was quite a responsibility, really. Because all I wanted was to please him and all he wanted was to please me. It's a wonder we went anywhere at all.

'When you say "base",' I began, 'what exactly are you thinking?'

'Somewhere safe that we can call home.'

'So we wouldn't go to the high mountains?'

'We might. Yes, of course. I really want to see them . . .'

'But Dog! If we went to the high mountains then that would be our home.'

'No! We'd only go to have a look.'

Have a look? There were times when I thought Dog and I lived on separate stars. I'd often looked up at those stars at night and thought how lonely they must be, all scattered across the black sky and never reaching each other. Well, when Dog told me some of the things that went on in his head, I felt as lonely as one of those stars.

'What is the point of having a look?' I asked him.

'To see,' he replied.

'What is the point of seeing, if you don't want to be there?'

'To know.'

'To know what, Dog?' I was beginning to feel irritable. I suppose I must have been getting better.

'To know what's there,' he replied.

I couldn't get it. I couldn't see the point.

'You're seriously suggesting that we should go all the way to the high mountains, open our eyes, have a look and then come all the way back again?' I couldn't stop the tone of my voice from showing that I thought he'd gone sun-crazy.

'But, Little,' he said in a dreamy, sort of straining voice, 'the high mountains are capped with white stuff that shines in the morning light. It comes in the late year and it almost disappears in summer. Humans call it "snow". I heard two of them talking about it once at the table place. "Look at the snow" one of them said. "Look at the snow on the Sierra." The other human turned round in her chair and looked up at the high mountains, shading her eyes with a hand. "Oh!" she sighed. "How I'd love to be in all that cool!" I wanted to know what they meant by it. I wanted to know snow and to feel the cool. And I always have, ever since.' He looked away, staring through the night up to the dark outline of the mountains on the distant horizon.

When he was in that mood he could almost break my heart. He had such a big mind. He wanted such difficult things.

I reached out and touched his cheek with my paw, so that he looked round at me. His eyes were shining and his mouth was open a little so that I could see the tip of his tongue.

'I want to know snow as well, Dog,' I whispered.

He looked at me for a long moment, then. He seemed almost puzzled. 'I think you will,' he said at last.

'Then we both will,' I told him cheerfully.

He continued to stare at me thoughtfully, then he yawned and scratched his neck. 'You wait till you see the village,' he said.

Chapter Fourteen

We set out early one morning a few days later. I was feeling much stronger by then and I was excited by the idea of moving on. Living with Dog was making me into quite a traveller. I was even beginning to wonder if I might not want to go all the way to the high mountains myself – just to see snow. Though I did think we ought to check if there'd be any food when we got there. We would be awfully hungry after all that walking.

As we left our nest, I couldn't help looking back to that corner of the road further down the valley. It was there that I'd almost lost the will to live and it was there that, soon after, Dog and I had found each other again. Whatever happens in life, I thought, however awful things may seem to be, it's always worth hanging on. You never know what may be coming for you; what may be just round the corner, out of sight. Like Dog had been out of sight to me that evening – until quite suddenly he was there in front of me and we were able to be together again.

The road wound up and down the side of the valley. It became much more hilly the higher we climbed. The valley itself seemed to divide into a number of smaller valleys, all pointing more or less uphill, then branching off in different directions.

We kept getting glimpses of the village. There were a lot of human houses of different sizes. Some had trees and flowers in front of them, surrounded by high walls. Most of the buildings were painted white. They were so bright in the sunlight that they dazzled the eyes. The houses were different heights and were built on different levels of the hillside. But they weren't separate. They all seemed joined together into one shape and formed a strange pattern of light and shade, glaring white and black shadows. In the middle of all this jumble of roofs and windows there was a square tower sticking up with a pointed red-tiled roof on top. Dog said it was a church.

'That's the thing that has the bell, Little,' he explained, 'the one we could hear clanging from the nest by the road.'

I wanted to ask him what a church was for. There was one down by the big water as well. Humans used to go to it in their best clothes. I didn't know why they went. There was a funny sweet smell from inside and bells and mumbling voices. I didn't know what the point of it was. But I thought it wiser not to ask Dog. I didn't want to risk annoying him, because I don't think he would have known the answer.

As we got closer, the road got steeper. We came to a place where a green valley veered away from us, running below the village and then widening out as it climbed up the other side of the houses. Dog led the way into this valley.

'Aren't we going straight to the village?' I asked. I was disappointed. I'd been looking forward to some human food and then a nice long sleep in the shade.

'We must make our nest first,' Dog said, trotting ahead of me up a narrow, grassy path.

The grass here still had a little green in it and there were seed heads of every size and pattern hanging above us which moved and shook as we pushed past them. Further off, through a narrow gorge, there were trees and bushes, which suggested that there must be spring water somewhere up ahead.

I was lagging a little way behind. I suppose I was getting tired. It was the first long journey I'd made since my illness. I was fussed that Dog wasn't waiting for me and was just about to call out to tell him to go slower, when I saw him suddenly stop in his tracks. I hurried my steps and soon caught him up. But I was wary as I did so. I could see the bristles standing up on the back of his neck. That usually meant danger.

'What is it?' I whispered. But before he had a chance to reply I smelled what he must have smelled to make him recoil so violently. The smell was so awful that I pulled back also, wanting to protect myself against this unknown peril.

It's difficult to describe a smell. But the one we met that day in the valley below the village was as near as I can imagine to what the experience of agony must smell like. Fear has a smell – and there was fear in it. But it was much worse than that. It smelled of humans at their most horrible. It smelled, I suddenly realized, just like the house of the man with the gun. It was also the smell of fox and the smell of terror and the smell of human machines and plastic – that never-having-lived, never-going-away kind of smell. And then, over and above all these smells, there was another one: the smell of death.

'What is it?' I gasped. 'Where is it coming from?'

It didn't take us long to find out. And I had been right, there was fox in the smell – dead fox.

The poor creature was stretched out, rigid on the ground, with its front paws reaching ahead of its body – almost as if it had tried to run away from some physical torture it had been suffering; to run away from itself. There was a look of such pain on its face, of such overwhelming agony. I wanted to reach out and touch it; to comfort it. But I couldn't bring myself to go near. Flies were buzzing round the corpse and settling on its open mouth. But it was the smell that affected us most. It was all enveloping. It filled the air and made us cough and choke.

'What's happened to it, Dog?' I whispered, gasping for breath.

'Come away, Little,' Dog growled. He was obviously very shaken.

'What happened to it?' I asked again after we had run a long way from the terrible body and felt safe enough to rest among some tall grasses. 'How did it die like that? What could have hurt it so much? What was that smell, Dog? What was it?'

'I don't know,' Dog replied. Then he was silent. He had that faraway look that I was to come to recognize over the months that followed and he was shaking.

'It's all right,' I told him, alarmed by his distress and wanting to reassure him. 'Whatever it was, the fox is dead now, so the suffering it experienced is over.'

But I couldn't get the stench out of my nostrils and I felt sick for most of the rest of that day. I think Dog must have had the same reaction. He was certainly very quiet and he had that faraway look in his eyes.

In fact from that day I think there was always a tiny bit of sadness in Dog. It wasn't always evident; just sometimes. It was as if he half knew something and the knowledge was nagging at him to be understood. Whatever it was – and I certainly had no idea what it could be – he would never speak about it and denied its presence when I asked him. But there was a sadness in him. A tiny fraction of fear that would bubble up to the surface of his mind and make him – on odd occasions and only for brief moments – look with that distant expression and that almost tragic half-awareness that I sometimes saw. I'm sure it was the smell of that fox that was haunting him and that it continued to do so from that time onwards.

That night we made our nest in the wooded glade at the end of the valley. There was water there, as I had guessed, and we were able to refresh ourselves after the rigours of the day. But we didn't go off to find food. We both pretended that we were too tired to bother. But I think really the memory of the dead fox and the foul man-made smell that surrounded it had taken away our appetites.

As we were settling down we could hear the sounds of the village distantly above us drifting on the evening air. Human voices and music playing.

'We'll go and explore in the morning,' Dog said, and he turned his back on me as though he were going to sleep.

But I could tell by his breathing that he was lying there with his eyes open.

'What are you thinking about?' I asked him later.

'Oh, just about life,' he replied.

I knew he was thinking about death; about the dead fox, lying rotting further down the path. I moved closer to him then and felt the warmth of his body against my own.

'I love you, Dog,' I whispered. But he didn't answer.

71

We didn't very often say it. But I wanted to that night. I wanted him to know. And I wanted to hear myself saying it.

'I love you,' I whispered again and I pressed my body against his as though I wanted to get inside him and to become part of him.

Chapter Fifteen

The next morning, when I awoke, Dog was already up and drinking water at the spring. He seemed altogether recovered from the night before and was in an excited, cheerful mood.

'Now, Little,' he said, running up to me and yelping and jumping round me, his tail wagging, 'this is where we're going to live. It's a good place and the water is sweet.'

'Aren't we going to the village?' I asked, lapping some water and aware of how hungry I was feeling.

'Yes, of course! We're going now. But this is our safe place. This is where we'll come to hide if we get into any scrapes.'

Scrapes? I don't know where he got the words. The fact that he listened so much to humans talking can be the only explanation. I suppose he'd have called being shot at by the man with the gun a 'scrape'. I thought a scrape was the raw bit of flesh you got after you'd rubbed against a jagged rock. It didn't exactly bleed, but it was sore to the touch – and the best remedy was to lick it better. That's what I thought a scrape was.

'So where will we sleep?' I asked.

'That depends on what we find. If there's a good place up there, then we might sleep there. But . . . Little, are you listening to me?'

I nodded. I was listening, but I really wanted to get going. I was hungry.

'We're going among humans,' he continued. The tone of his voice made my heart race. He was making me scared. 'Humans are tricky creatures. With a cat or a fox you know where you are. But humans keep changing. They can be nice to you one moment and turn horrible the next—'

'Excuse me, Dog,' I interrupted. 'I may be younger than you are but I have known quite a lot of humans. And I know exactly how to behave. Even when they're being nice to you, a bit of you has to be ready to run. Even if you're asleep near them you have to keep half an eye on them. The good thing is they're very slow runners themselves and they're absolutely hopeless at crawling through low openings or at scrambling up and over high walls. So it isn't too difficult to get away from them—'

'And the bad thing about them,' Dog now interrupted me, using his most severe voice, 'is that they have guns and other machines. You can't run faster than a gunshot. And we've seen enough squashed creatures to know how dangerous their cars can be.'

My tail went down and I hung my head – because he was right, of course. Humans without doubt are the most dangerous animals a dog is likely to meet. Even the good ones can be clumsy and step on you when they're not looking.

'I don't know why we're going to the beastly village then,' I said in a sulky voice.

74

'Because it's an adventure!' he barked, and he raced away up the path and then skidded round and raced back towards me, his tail wagging. 'All I'm saying is — be sure to get to know the path as we're going along, so that you can find it again in an emergency.'

An emergency! He certainly knew how to make a dog feel cheerful! But, yet again, I knew what he was saying was right. I whimpered quietly and put my head on one side. But he just grinned and wagged his tail.

'If anything happens,' he continued, 'if we lose each other or one of us has to make a dash for it, this is where we must look for each other.'

'You mean if I go paddling up a river and you lose my scent, don't you? That's what you're getting at. You mean if I do something stupid . . .' I felt he was picking on me.

'No! It's me as well. Who led us right to the door of that human with the gun? And would have gone on, if you hadn't barked and stopped me? We have to be extra careful, that's all I'm saying. This is where we must come in an emergency. It's very important that you remember that, Little. I don't — ever — want us to lose each other again.'

I nodded and looked serious. 'I'll be sure to watch and smell every inch of the way,' I told him.

It was a steep climb. First on a very narrow path with high grasses and seed heads on either side. Then we crossed a stony field, which smelled of humans and other dogs. After that we were on a broader track, one that humans use. In fact this track began to smell more and more of humans the further we went along it. It curved round a long bend and we could see the village just a little way in front of us, getting closer with every step we took. Finally, at the top of a steep bank and next to a human building, like magic the track turned into a hard road.

This road went in two directions. Sloping upwards it was clear that it was going away from the village. Sloping downwards we could see the first of the houses.

'We're on the edge of the village,' Dog whispered. He liked telling me things – even when they were obvious.

So, with my heart pounding and my legs feeling a bit weak from nervous excitement, we entered the village.

The first thing we noticed was a door in a wall. The road split into two and branched away on either side of it. The door was open and inside we could see a funny wedge-shaped room with chairs and little tables and a counter that had bottles and jars on it. There were a few humans in the room and they were all drinking from glasses and laughing and talking. When we looked in they didn't bother to notice us – which was a very good sign. The best humans for a dog in the wild are the ones who take no notice of you. You can nip in and take the odd scraps from them and they don't really bother about you.

There was a tall man at the counter. He wasn't drinking, but he was talking and then he came out, carrying some squares of paper in his hand. (Later I would discover these were called 'the post', and apparently the post could sometimes be good and sometimes not so good.) This man did take notice of us. He stopped and bent down and put his hand out to me, making a funny clicking sound – as if he were saying 'hello' in some strange language. I pulled away from him at once and Dog and I ran round a corner out of his sight, just to be on the safe side. When, later, I peeped back, curious to see what was happening, the man was walking away up the narrow street with his back to me, looking at the post.

I was actually seeing David for the first time, but I didn't know it then and I'm sure he will never remember that that was our first meeting.

We went along the other road that day. Maybe if we'd followed David we would have come to the magic garden a lot sooner, but it wasn't to be. Instead we got to know the lower part of the village and it was only later that we came to the brown door in the white wall that was to change our lives for ever.

The village seemed on the whole quite friendly. There were a few dogs that were a bit fierce and there was one place – a shop in a narrow lane with high houses on either side – where the human was far from welcoming and clapped her hands and made horrible shooing noises. This was really annoying because inside the shop the smells were delicious. Dog was so hungry himself by now that he decided to try to get back in. He was brave, Dog! Actually, he could be brave to a fault. Many's the time I watched him with my heart pounding as though it would burst. This time was a perfect example. Dog darted into the shop, thinking it was empty, and the next thing I saw, he was charging out again followed by a deluge of water. The human had been mopping the floor, and catching Dog approaching she'd emptied her bucket on him. I actually thought it served him right. It made me laugh so much, seeing him running out all soaking and cross, that I had to sit down in the street.

We eventually had a good meal out of a plastic bag that was dumped with a lot of other bags and rubbish around a number of big bins. Then we went off into the open country not far from these bins and slept away the hot afternoon under some bushes.

'Not a bad first day!' Dog yawned.
'Was the water nice and cool?' I giggled.
'Go to sleep, Little,' he growled.

Chapter Sixteen

Our life in the village soon settled into a pattern not unlike our life had been down by the big water. There were enough humans about to supply us with scraps. There was fresh water in several different places. And we'd made a nest for ourselves in the open country near the bins.

From the nest we could see right down the valley. The ground dropped away in a series of dusty ridges. Nearer to us, humans had dug fields and were trying to grow crops of vegetables – though the ground seemed too stony and dry for them to have much success. There were a few trees that grew hard little nuts later in the year. Much further away, down the steep slopes, we could see the plastic place. It was larger than I'd thought and covered the whole of the valley bottom. The plastic houses looked more like sheets of water than anything else. Strange, square lakes of a dull, grey colour that reflected the light – like stagnant puddles. In the farthest distance, beyond the plastic, the valley ended in a wedge of blue that merged into the blue of the sky. That was the big water and we could even see tiny human houses clustered beside it.

I would spend hours lying under the bushes near our nest, just staring down at that view. That's where we've come from, I used to think. It was like seeing our entire lives spread out in front of us. Somewhere down there Mother and the one remaining brother and my sisters might still be living in the yard. Somewhere down there was the first nest that Dog and I shared and the table place and the water channel. You could, in certain lights, actually see the road – though you couldn't really make out the lorries on it, even though I tried to persuade myself I could. Then there was the plastic place; it was so vast that it had taken us a two-day walk to get through it. Then, somewhere in the scramble of dull browns and yellows that made up the land, there was the house of the man with the gun, and the river and the place where I'd waited for Dog under the dusty trees. I couldn't make out the water-glade that I'd shared with the birds but the narrow road was visible winding its way up to the village. On one of those distant bends Dog and I had been reunited. My heart would beat fast just remembering. I'd been so lucky. If I hadn't been on the road at that precise moment when he was passing by then I might have missed him for ever.

The whole of my life until now has been spent in that valley, I would think; it's spread out there for me to see. That's the past and I can remember every moment of it. But of course the future is different; the future is a dark mystery, out of sight and totally unknown until it comes to pass.

Or it certainly was for me. But now, sometimes, when I look back I almost believe that Dog could see the future as well. Not very clearly, but sort of glimpses of it – like the village had kept coming into view and then disappearing again behind folds in the land as we followed the twisting road up towards it.

And in that way of his he could recognize our next move and know what direction we should take.

'I think we should move higher up,' he said one night.

Higher up? Were we talking mountains here? I sighed and it was a sound that was more like a groan. I knew it had been too good to last; all this lying about, dreaming and not having to worry.

'There's a place above the village where the water flows all the time and the trees and bushes are more leafy. It gets so hot here, don't you think?'

Oh! If he was only talking about moving nest, that was all right! I didn't mind that one little bit. I quite enjoyed making a new nest. But: 'What about food?' I said. We were nice and handy for the bins where we were.

'I think we should explore.' Dog yawned and scratched himself. 'If we could find some friendly humans, they might give us fresh scraps regularly, like the house dogs get; or failing that, at least we could raid their bins. The food in the bins here isn't exactly fresh, you must admit. But, you decide, Little. It was only a thought . . .' And he dozed off to sleep in mid sentence.

House dogs! It was the first time I'd heard him use that expression. But it was a good one. The dogs that didn't live in the wild, like us, were each attached to a particular human and to that human's house. I couldn't imagine what that must be like. I suspect at the time the idea didn't really appeal to me – I liked my freedom too much. But that suggestion of regular supplies of fresh scraps was tempting.

We set off through the village in the early evening. It was really the best time for travelling because it was cooler, and with any luck we could pick up something to eat along the way, which would save us an extra journey. As usual we had to run through the main square. That place always made me nervous. Old humans sit there, talking, with smoking tubes in their mouths. Sometimes, in those days, they would throw things at us: pebbles or an empty tin. I don't think the humans really wanted us here. Maybe they thought there were too many dogs in the village already. The dogs also hung around the square and they often used to chase us and were none too friendly themselves. (I expect they didn't want outsiders moving into their territory either. I can understand that. There is only so much food to go round and they have to look after their own interests. But what were we supposed to do if we hadn't got a home and didn't belong anywhere? We had to live somewhere.)

After the square, we went as far as the church – having to really race past the place where the woman had poured water over Dog. She hated us. But that's not surprising either. Several times we'd both been into her place and got away with quite good pickings, which made her mad! From the church we struck off on a higher path; one I'd never been on before. Dog probably had. He was such an explorer that everywhere I went you can be sure he'd been before. We passed through a small open area, with a few trees. There were seats here, hanging on ropes, and human children used to swing on them sometimes. We climbed a steep little hill and came to another rough lane. We could go one of two ways here. Dog stopped and was sniffing the ground, trying to make up his mind which direction to take. I just sat down and waited for him. He was always the track finder.

There was a high white wall along the side of this lane. It had trees and brightly coloured flowering bushes peeping over the top of it. I'd just stretched out in the dust and rolled over on my back for a scratch when I heard the *click* of a door opening. Quickly rolling onto my stomach – ready to spring away if it seemed necessary – I saw a door in the white wall, which I hadn't noticed before, swing open.

It was a dark-brown door. It was wide, not like the usual house doors. I don't know why, but as soon as I saw it swinging open I ran towards it. This was so unlike me. I was usually the one who waited to be sure before I went rushing in. But I wanted to see what was on the other side of that door.

As I reached it, a woman came out. She was followed by a small dog and a man. It was the man I'd seen on the day we first arrived in the village.

He closed the door in the wall and hurried to catch up with the woman. They had their backs to me, walking away towards a distant corner and hadn't noticed me crouching at the side of the lane. But the dog looked back. She wagged her tail and barked once, with her head tilted questioningly. Then she ran out of sight, round the corner – hurrying after the humans.

I didn't know then, of course, but they were Joanna and David. And the dog, their dog, had a name of her own – she was called Fanny, I would later discover. They were going out for their evening walk. But all that information, that whole pattern of life, was in the unknown future for me then and I don't think I was even interested in it – or them. Not at the time.

I was totally caught up with the view I'd glimpsed through the brown door. There was a car parked immediately inside the door and beyond it I'd seen a path winding up towards the most beautiful great bushes, covered with flowers. It was as if there was a secret place beyond the wall: a whole landscape with a hill and a winding track that led to a higher level that you couldn't even guess at until you went through the door. On the other side of that white wall I'd glimpsed an entirely new world. The scent of that world that had gushed out of the open door before the man closed it was so strong and so delicious, you could have drunk it and thought yourself in paradise.

'Oh, Dog!' I barked, running back to him. 'I've just seen the most wonderful place. Behind this wall, there's . . .' I barked again and then was silent. I couldn't describe what I'd just smelled and seen. It was a magic garden. The place of my dreams.

That night we ate scraps and then made a temporary nest in a corner of the place with the swing seats. I wasn't happy about this. I felt we were too out in the open. But we were both tired and hadn't been able to find anywhere better. We were surrounded by narrow lanes and houses and there was nowhere to shelter. The only alternative would have been to go back to our old nest. But that would have meant going all the way through the village and we didn't feel up to that sort of journey.

As we were getting ready for sleep I told Dog again about the view through the door. I don't think he'd been listening the first time. He was very impressed and I rather enjoyed the fact that I'd seen it first.

'That's the sort of place we're looking for, Little,' he said. 'That's where we want to live.'

'But how?' I asked.

'I've been thinking about that a lot recently,' Dog said, sitting up and having a good scratch with a back paw. 'How can we get some humans to take us in?'

'Is that what we want?' I asked. I was very surprised at the idea. It didn't sound like Dog at all.

'Look at us, Little. We're both thin. We need proper food. That's what humans are for. This is a good place; but not for dogs in the wild. We're not welcome here. You've seen how they treat us. But for house dogs it's quite different.'

'You mean we're going to be house dogs? Oh, Dog! You're pretending!'

'I know it must sound like that. But . . . why not? Why shouldn't we be house dogs and never have to worry about where our next meal is coming from? Why not, Little?'

'Because you'd never take to it. You'd hate to be shut in.'

'But what about you?'

'I'm not going to be a house dog on my own, so don't you try to make me.' But even as I was protesting I was thinking about the humans and their dog who lived behind the big brown door. That dog had looked so happy. 'Besides, how could we ever get humans to take us in?'

'It's up to you. You'll have to be very nice to them.'

'Why me?'

'Oh, Little!' Dog yawned. 'Why d'you think?'

'I don't know, do I?'

'Because you're you. You can make humans like you.'

But they grew to like him too. If only he could have known how much. I have been popular with humans, I admit that. They think I'm pretty and they like to pet me. But Dog was the one they enjoyed being with really. Dog was the one who was fun. Dog was always the favourite.

Chapter Seventeen

We stayed in and around the place with the swinging seats for much longer than we intended. It was meant only to be a temporary resting place, until we found somewhere better. But because it was close to the brown door, it looked as if it was becoming our permanent home. I began to wonder if we hadn't been better off at our nest near the bins. At least there was some cover from the weather and a bit of security there. But Dog had set his sights on the brown door and he could be very determined.

We got to know a woman in a house nearby who started to put out scraps for us. She always left them in the same place and we got into the habit of waiting there for her. She was really nice and once or twice I let her stroke me. She had a man who seemed friendly as well. I suggested to Dog that maybe we should try to move in with them; the food was good and their house had a walled garden which looked cool when we glimpsed it through the open door. As the summer sun beat down, any shade in our corner by the swing seats had become almost non-existent and I think Dog was half inclined to agree with me. But he didn't want to give up the idea of getting inside the magic garden.

Then, quite suddenly, one day the woman and her man

went away. They brought out a lot of big square boxes with handles, which they put into their car. Then the man locked the door of the house and he and the woman got into the car and drove off down the narrow lane.

We were very worried. We sensed they wouldn't be coming back for some time. They'd had a look that we both recognized: that determined light in the eyes that comes when you're about to set off on a journey.

'Just when we'd got used to them,' I muttered. 'We'll have to start hunting for scraps all over again.'

But that night Joanna came down and put out food for us. It was as though she knew the other woman had gone and had decided that she would feed us instead.

As soon as we saw her coming we scuttled away into hiding. Then we watched her as she emptied a bag of scraps and looked round as if she were trying to see us.

The food she left was delicious and we would have eaten it twice over, given the chance. But we were puzzled about why it had happened. Was she going to feed us from now on? Would she come regularly or was this just a passing whim on her part? It was difficult to know. We talked about the possibilities late into the night.

What bothered me was that I'd never before known humans who went out of their way to help us. Now, suddenly, we'd met two in quick succession.

'It might be a trap,' I grumbled. 'Why would they want to help us?'

'Maybe they've taken pity on us,' Dog growled quietly.

'Humans don't do that. They might throw you a scrap onto the ground in the table place. But they wouldn't get up from their chair and make the effort of finding you and giving you the scrap . . .'

'Maybe it's different here.'

'Yes – but for how long?' I whined. 'We'll just start to get used to it and it'll stop. Look how that other woman has just gone off . . .'

'And this one has come instead. Maybe the other woman told her she was going away . . . Maybe it was all arranged.'

'Maybe! Maybe! We can't live by maybe . . .'

'Oh, Little! Go to sleep! You see a catch in everything!'

'It was you who said we had to be on our guard. It was you who said we couldn't be too careful. I'm not sure we wouldn't be better off back down in that valley in our scrape-nest,' I nagged, and I would have gone on if Dog's deep breathing hadn't told me that I'd sent him off to sleep.

'All the same, it was a good sign, Little,' Dog said the following day.

'What was?'

'That it was her of all people who should have come to feed us.'

We were lying in the shade, discussing yet again what had happened. I was feeling decidedly low. I'd got used to the other woman feeding us and I didn't like the way she'd just gone away. That's the trouble with humans: they're not at all reliable – not to a dog in the wild.

'I don't see why you call it a good sign,' I grumbled. I was doing a lot of that – grumbling – and although I longed to stop, I just couldn't. I think maybe we'd been living rough for too long, without even a nest to call our own.

'It means she wants to help us,' Dog insisted. 'And she's the one who lives in the magic garden, don't forget.'

88

'Bringing us a few scraps doesn't mean she wants us to go and live there with her,' I whined. 'Apart from anything else, they already have a house dog.'

Dog scratched himself and stared at the high white wall. 'Must be plenty of room behind there for the three of us,' he said and, as he was speaking, he got up and trotted along the lane.

'Where are you going?' I asked, running after him.

'Just an idea,' he said. 'Come on.'

We ran, via several different lanes, right up to the top of the village. Here there was a long human building with a trough in front of it. There was water running into the trough from a spout in the wall.

I'd been to this place a few times with Dog. He'd suggested we should move here when we decided to leave the bins. I thought it quite a good place but it was a bit far from any regular supply of food.

'Why have we come here?' I asked, as we both lapped from the spout.

'Just an idea,' he replied, letting the water run over his head and then shaking himself dry.

Dog and his ideas could sometimes be rather irritating. I think he enjoyed keeping me guessing what it was he was planning.

Once we were refreshed, we continued to run along the high lane in the direction of the open country. The village was spread out below us, down steeply sloping ground.

Eventually Dog led the way off the lane into a rough field. He started sniffing and darting about. I was used to this behaviour by then. It meant he was track finding. I just sat down and waited.

'Come on!' he barked eventually, and he sounded really excited.

I followed him to the edge of the field. Here the ground dropped away, almost sheer. There was a jumble of stunted trees and bushes and tall, thick plants. He pushed his way through all this vegetation, with me just behind him – complaining of course! It was a warm, thundery day with a gusty breeze that made the air feel hot and sticky. There were also some bothersome flies buzzing round my head that I longed to catch.

'There!' Dog whispered. He had stopped right on the edge of a line of stones. It was the top of a wall, set against the steep side of the hill, and there was a long drop in front of us.

We were looking down through a tracery of branches onto the side of a white house and a section of garden. The walls of the house were covered with blossom. There was a brilliant red-purple flowering creeper growing up a corner. It was so tall that its branches reached right to the roof. It wound through the railing of a balcony on an upstairs window, its thick stem twisting round the bars. Next to it was a great jumble of stalks, like green wires, covered with tiny leaves and white star-shaped flowers. Then a shower of the palest yellow petals on thorny stems. More white flowers intertwined with the yellow and a pale-blue star flower grew in amongst the white.

The walls of the house were so thickly covered with growth that at first you scarcely noticed the open windows with white curtains, billowing in the breeze.

I had never seen so many flowers! This riot of colour and growth spread right along the wall beneath our feet. There were also a number of trees. One very large one was almost in front of us. It had shiny green fruit hanging on it – like huge drops of dark water.

The scent that rose from the garden was like a perfumed dream. It was every nice smell that you could imagine all rolled into one. Flowers and honey; cool shade smells and hot grasses; moisture and lemons; and – most important for a dog in the wild, perhaps the best of all smells – that comforting, faint hint of human food.

'It's the place, isn't it?' I whispered. I could hardly believe my eyes. 'It's the magic garden.'

Then, before Dog had a chance to answer, I saw the house dog trot into view. She stretched her legs in a lazy way and wandered over to the cool shade of some bushes. Pleased with the place she had chosen, she flopped down, curled into a heap and, with a contented sigh, went to sleep.

I wanted to be that dog so much. I wanted to trot round the side of the house and choose a nice cool spot for a doze. I wanted to stand at the gate and bark at strangers. I wanted to have secret places under the flowers that only I knew about. I wanted to know that the garden and the house and the humans that lived there were all mine. I wanted to belong there and to know that I could stay there for ever.

It was a terrible wanting. It actually hurt. It had a pain in it that seemed to cut into my chest and made me gasp. I'd never actually wanted anything so desperately before. Not like that. I'd been content to wait to see what would happen next. Dog would, eventually, have taken me all the way to the high mountains, I think. But not any more. I'd found where I wanted to be for the rest of my life.

'Oh, Dog!' I whispered. 'Why can't we live down there? Why are we outsiders? Why is that dog so lucky? Did she do something to make her deserve her life? If so, Dog, I'll do whatever it is that's required. Why do we have to be hungry and scared all the time? Why, Dog?'

He didn't answer me. He just leaned against me, staring down. I could feel his body trembling. I think he was wanting as well.

Chapter Eighteen

Joanna came and fed us each evening and we remained sleeping in the corner of the swing place. The routine continued much as before. The only slight change we made was that we now waited for our scraps outside the brown door and she would put them in a corner of the lane just across from it.

Each time Joanna came out through the brown door we got a tantalizing view of the lower garden. It was obvious that the winding path led up a hill to a higher level and it was there that the house stood, with its covering of sweet-smelling flowers. It did seem a huge world between that white wall and the high drop that we'd discovered. I began to think that Dog was right. There was plenty of room in there for us to live without disturbing the house dog. We could just make ourselves a little nest somewhere out of the way. She'd hardly be aware of us. Joanna could come and feed us each evening and everything would be perfect.

But how? How could we get them to let us in?

Joanna spoke to us often when she brought the food but she used the same funny language that the other woman had done and I couldn't understand what she was saying. Her voice was soft and quiet – not at all like the voices of the humans where we'd lived beside the big water, or like most of the humans in the village. Perhaps these kind women who liked to feed us were also outsiders? I didn't know. It was all very confusing.

I'd noticed this different way of talking before — at the table place. There were a lot of different humans who came to eat there and sometimes there'd be several languages all being spoken at once. It seems an unnecessary complication to me. We dogs all speak the same. No matter which village a dog comes from he can be understood. We'd travelled all the way from the big water to the village in the hills but we understood what the dogs were saying to us. (Not very nice things, usually.) We dogs manage perfectly well with one language but humans always have to complicate matters.

Dog said that all I had to do was to listen and that I'd soon pick up what she was saying. He said it was very important that I should learn her language, because she'd want me to be obedient.

Obedient? What was that? Some new notion of Dog's? I don't know how his head didn't explode with all the ideas that were crammed into it.

But try as I might I wasn't getting anywhere with Joanna's language. It just didn't make sense. She could have been asking me to come into the magic garden for all I knew. (Though if she had been she'd have held the brown door open for me and then I'd have run in even if she hadn't said a single word.) I knew that usually she was saying nice things to me because of her tone — which was friendly and gentle — but as to what it was she was trying to tell me I hadn't a clue.

Dog said that that was the secret of understanding, he thought. You didn't need to know what every word meant, you had to listen to the thoughts behind the words instead.

He said a lot of things, Dog! Now that I understand so much more myself I wish he was here so that I could argue with him. In those days every mad idea of his went unchallenged by me. But he was right about the language. One day I just, quite suddenly, understood what they were saying – and I've continued to do so ever since.

That particular day was quite a special one for another reason, actually. It was the first time I set foot in the magic garden.

We'd returned to The View. That's what we called the top of the high wall. It had become a favourite place of ours and we went quite often. It was a long walk but worth it once we were there. The bushes gave us pleasant shade from the sun and just to look down into the garden reminded us how good and beautiful our dream was.

But dreams can be tantalizing and I was getting to the point where I wanted more than a view of the garden. I wanted to be in it.

I remember it was cruelly hot that day and that both of us were irritable. The summers are so long that they wear you down and you can be a bit bad tempered even with the dog you love.

We were lying under our favourite bush, which gave us the best view of all. I think I'd probably already worked out what I was going to do long before it happened. But it still came as a surprise to me when I put it to the test.

Maybe it was the heat that caused it to happen – it can make you do the strangest things. But suddenly, then and there, I was determined to get into that garden. I'd had enough of being an outsider. I didn't want to be looking in any more. I wanted to wander about in it and push my nose into all the flowers and smell all the different scents and scramble through the bushes and see round the corners.

I already knew how I'd do it. Over all the weeks we'd been visiting The View I'd worked out the route I'd take. Getting in wasn't going to be a problem. If you can jump – which all dogs can – then jumping downwards is much easier than jumping up.

No – the problem would be getting out again! That was what kept us lying up on the edge of the high wall. That was what prevented us venturing down into our dream world. Once down there, we'd be trapped.

But on that day I decided to worry about getting out after I was in. Who could tell? There might be quite an easy way out which we couldn't see until we were down there.

Dog was lying panting. It was too hot for sleep. When I got up and stretched he didn't even bother to move. He had no idea what I was up to, of course.

I went to the edge of the wall and looked over. There was a short drop, then a broad ledge which had a few trees and bushes growing on it. After that there was a much longer drop, down to the brown and bleached short grass of the garden.

I took a breath, glanced over my shoulder at Dog and yelped quietly. 'I'm going down,' I said. Then I jumped before Dog had a chance to stop me.

I landed on the second ledge, scrambled to the edge, then I launched myself over the side.

I was falling and flying and I could feel the wind catching in the hairs of my coat. I expect it only took an instant but it seemed a very long and terrifying time before I landed with a thud on the ground.

For a moment I just lay there, my heart racing. Then I stood up and shook myself. I looked up. It was a cliff I'd come down! It made me giddy just looking up. At the top I could see Dog, craning over, searching for me, a worried expression on his face.

I barked once — just to let him know I was all right. But as I did so, I must have woken the house dog. She came tearing round the corner of the house, barking wildly and growling.

She was no bigger than I was and I thought she was probably considerably older. But I wasn't prepared to get in a fight with her — not on her home territory. So I turned tail and fled.

I came to a gap in a wall. But there was an iron gate barring my exit. It was made of upright poles and through it I could see a big square pool of bright blue water, with a white wall beyond it. The light on the water and on the wall was so brilliant that I had to half close my eyes.

Then the dog came up behind me again. She was still barking and in a furious temper. She didn't want uninvited guests in her garden, that was the problem.

I ducked away from her through a gap in a hedge and found myself in a long, narrow bit of garden. There was a tree with yellow fruit on it. Beyond was a low wall, thick with flowering shrubs. I dashed to the wall, thinking I'd leap over. But, landing precariously on its top, I found myself looking down an incredibly long way to the ground far below. In a flash I saw a huge square of soil girdled by a high wall. There were bright creepers against the wall and the soil area was filled with plants and bushes. Then I saw the roof of a car — only it was more like a van, really. It was parked in front of a big brown door in the wall. I knew at once that I was looking down on the inside of the white wall: beyond that door I'd had my first, tantalizing glimpse of the magic garden. I saw the sloping track, coming up from the parked van and going round a corner just below me. It would, I reckoned, eventually arrive at the big blue pool.

But I had only time for a quick look before the dog was snapping at me again. I jumped down off the wall and turned on her, spitting and growling. I only wanted to frighten her off. But she was no coward. She came at me with a savage yelp. I turned and ran.

I skidded out through another gap in the hedge and found myself standing in front of the house. There was a big porch, smothered in creeper. The ground-floor windows were closed. But there was a wide doorway — really two doors together — that was open. Through this door I saw a short passageway and then, beyond it, what looked like another garden. A cool square place, with filtered light and a few plants growing.

I was trying to decide which way to go when I heard a man's voice calling from above me.

'Fan!' he called — something like that. 'Fanny! Fan!'

At the same moment the dog hurled herself out of the hedge and came towards me. I turned and raced back onto the area of grass where I had first landed. In front of me was the sheer wall.

I was trapped!

In the nick of time I noticed, on the other side of the tree with the green fruit, that the wall had a few stones and rocks jutting out of it. I made a dash for it and started to scramble and jump and cling and climb from stone to stone up the sheer stone face.

I don't know how I did it. Fear, I suppose. But somehow I managed to reach the ledge.

'Cat!' I heard a woman exclaim.

'Where?' a man said.

'Went straight up that wall!'

I glanced back then from the safety of the ledge and saw them both leaning over the balcony of the room on the corner, surrounded by all the hectic reds of the flowering shrub.

'Dearest,' I heard the man say. 'Look! Up on the terrace. I think your cat might turn out to be one of the strays!'

'Oh!' the woman exclaimed. 'The naughty little thing! How did she get in?' Then she called out: 'Who's a good girl, Fanny! Was there a dog in your garden? No wonder you were cross!'

They were Joanna and David, of course. And Fanny was their house dog. But I still didn't know any of their names.

'A cat!' I barked, scrambling up the final bit of the cliff and reaching The View not far from our bush.

'She called me a cat!' I yelped to Dog, who was lying on his back, laughing. He thought it was the funniest thing he'd ever seen.

It was only later that it dawned on me that I'd understood every word that had been said.

Chapter Nineteen

Of course, the most important thing that happened that day – even more than being in the garden for the first time and understanding their language – was that they gave us names.

For a dog in the wild, a human name is a sign that they are getting used to seeing you. Once they're used to seeing you, you can start relaxing a bit. The next step is getting a name from them – a name is the first sign of being owned by them. When humans think they own you, you might eventually get inside their house and live with them.

Or that was Dog's theory.

It was later the same day – in the evening, immediately after my adventure in the garden. We'd gone back to the lane outside the brown door. We were always there at the same time, waiting for Joanna to bring our food. But this time we were a little nervous. Perhaps she'd be cross with us. David had recognized me. Maybe they wouldn't feed us, to punish me for going in their garden.

'That wouldn't be very fair on you,' I grumbled to Dog. 'You didn't go in the garden. They should feed you and punish me.'

'But if they did, I'd share the food with you, then you wouldn't be punished,' Dog said.

'They wouldn't know that,' I whined. 'You make it sound as though you think I should be punished.'

'You should have told me what you were going to do.'

'If I had, you'd have stopped me.'

'You could have been trapped, down in that garden.'

'You would have been,' I corrected him, tossing my ears. 'You can't climb nearly as well as I can.'

'No dog can,' he said, 'Well, none that I've ever seen. Maybe the human is right – maybe you have got some cat blood in you.'

He could make me really cross when he was teasing me. He knew I couldn't stand cats.

Then the door opened and Joanna came out, followed by David and Fanny. It was not a good sign, all of them being there.

As soon as Fanny saw me, she ran up to me. I shot away, thinking she'd still be angry. But she ran after me, barking and with her tail wagging. I looked over my shoulder, calling for Dog. But I couldn't see him. He'd obviously run off in another direction.

Fanny chased me all the way down to the place with the swing seats. She wasn't angry this time. Now it was a game she was playing. All the time David was calling her name and telling her to 'Come here!' But we raced about, ignoring him, as we dodged and darted, barking cheerfully.

Then, through all our noise and excitement, I heard Joanna calling as well. But she wasn't calling for Fanny. She was saying, 'Kitty! Don't be naughty! Leave Fanny alone. Come and have your supper. Kitty! Kitty!'

I didn't know what she meant. Who, or what, was 'Kitty'?

Fanny eventually gave up the game of chase and

returned to David, who'd come halfway down the hill to collect her.

'Come on, Fan,' he said – not sounding cross at all. Then he bent down and called to me, where I was skulking behind some stones. 'Kitty! You as well! Come on, Kitty! Have your supper, there's a good girl.' And he clapped his hands gently and seemed to beckon me. He had such a nice voice. I'd have followed him anywhere.

'Where are you going?' I called to Fanny, trotting after them back up the hill. I wasn't scared of her now we'd been playing together.

'For a walk,' she replied.

'What's a walk?' I asked.

'It's a thing humans need at least once a day,' Fanny called.

Dog was already eating the scraps when I got to him and Joanna was standing quite close.

'Oh, David! Look at this one. He's so thin,' she said, as he and Fanny came up. Fanny immediately tried to get the food and Dog snarled at her and snapped.

'Stop it, Fan! That's Bailey's supper. You'll get yours later.'

'Kitty!' Joanna said, bending down towards me. 'Eat your supper.'

Then, as I started to gobble the food – it had been a long and very exciting day and I was starving – Joanna and David turned and walked away from us, with Fanny trotting in front of them.

'They look half starved,' I heard Joanna say. Then she added, 'Why Bailey?'

'His colouring!' David replied. 'Who's the king of the black and whites?'

'Oh, I see! David Bailey!' Joanna said, and she laughed as they disappeared out of our hearing round the corner.

After scraps we always went for a drink to a place where water dribbled into a bowl from a spout in a wall. That evening Dog was jubilant.

'Well done, Little! Well done!' he kept saying – he was almost singing it, he was so pleased.

I love being praised but I need to know what I've done to deserve it. On this occasion I wasn't sure. It was only a little while earlier that he'd been ticking me off for going into the garden.

'But that was before I discovered how they'd take it,' Dog explained, as we lay side by side in our corner of the swing-seat place in what was fast becoming our permanent non-nest. (A real nest needs at least a bit of shelter. Here there was none.)

'How did they take it?' I asked.

'Oh, Kitty!' Dog growled. And then he rolled over on his back and laughed with his paws in the air.

'What did you call me?' I said, sitting up and staring down at him.

'Kitty.'

'Why?'

'That's the name they've given you.'

I put my head on one side and thought about it. 'What does it mean?'

'I don't know. I don't think names do "mean". I think they just "are".'

'Kitty!' I said, trying to get used to it. Then I remembered David's words. 'And Bailey!' I said.

Dog rolled over onto his tummy and looked up at me,

with his head on one side. 'He did, didn't he?' he asked, his eyes shining.

'What?'

'He did call me a name as well?'

He seemed so anxious. I wanted to hug him.

'If you can call Bailey a name,' I said.

His tail wagged furiously. Then stopped. Then wagged again. It was as if he couldn't quite trust what had happened.

'I knew they'd like you,' he said at last. 'I wasn't so sure about me. It's a good name, isn't it? Bailey? It sounds good.'

'It's all right,' I told him. 'But you'll always be Dog to me.'

'But a human name, Kitty. A human name!' Then he sighed and stretched out. 'It must mean they like us.'

'And she's Joanna and he's David and the dog is Fanny – or Fan? Which name? They seem to use both . . .'

Dog was lying on his side with a contented grin on his face.

'Dog, are you listening to me?' I said.

'No. Bailey is,' Dog said, and I could feel his tail wagging in the dust beside me.

'Bailey!' I said. 'You'll always be Dog to me.'

And he always was, in my heart.

Chapter Twenty

At the very beginning it was Fanny who encouraged Joanna and David to take more care of us. She'd probably deny this, but it's true. I think she was actually a bit lonely before we arrived. She needed to have some dogs to play with and to talk to.

I'm not surprised. If I'd been on my own, after I left Mother and my brother and sisters, I don't know how I'd have managed. Fanny, of course, had Joanna and David for company. (And I'd soon learn that a house dog's attitude to life is very different to ours.) But she had so much time on her own in the magic garden that she must sometimes have longed for another dog to chase, or just to potter about with; to be able to share smells and inspect things together.

Actually, although she'd always been a house dog, Fanny has had her share of unhappiness as well and this sometimes makes her a difficult dog to understand. She can be really nice to you one moment – then she can turn and be quite spiteful. But it doesn't usually last long and really I'd forgive her anything. When she's in one of her moods I've learned to hold my tongue and to keep out of her way. In fact, I think she has every right to be a bit moody. It isn't every dog that would have put up with us.

Maybe she does remember that she was responsible for persuading Joanna and David to ask us into the garden. Though when I suggested this to her not long ago, she simply growled and walked away from me. Fanny is one of those dogs who always has to be right and on that particular day she was a bit off me – I don't remember why. (Probably I was getting too much attention – that always annoys her.) Anyway, the last thing she wanted to admit was that she'd asked for us to be there!

But she did.

She started refusing to go for her walk with Joanna and David until we'd finished our scraps and we could all go together. She'd sit at the end of the lane and not budge, no matter how much David called her. She didn't try to eat our food or anything like that, she just sat and waited.

She didn't have to wait long, of course. Dogs are not like humans. Humans can sit eating a meal for *hours*. They pause all the time – to talk. They sit there, chattering away, with the food in front of them. They push it about, with things called a knife and fork, and mash it and cut it and turn it . . . To watch a human eat is one of the most irritating experiences for a dog. Of course the reason they behave like that is they have far too much food; they're not really interested in it – or even hungry. Also, other humans don't come and steal it away – at least I don't think they do. We dogs eat fast because we're starving. We don't need to talk while we're feeding – there's all the rest of the day for that. And we have to get it down quickly, in case some other creature comes along and takes it. I've even known Dog try to 'help me out' (his words) on occasions. 'Help me out? I don't need any help, thank you!' I'd growl and I'd nip his nose if he got too close.

So we'd usually finished our scraps before Joanna and David had reached the end of the lane. Then Fanny would bark, 'Come on!'

'She wants us to follow,' Dog said, the first time it happened.

'Why?' I asked, licking a paw.

'I suppose she wants to play,' he said.

Playing on a full stomach isn't much fun. Fanny, I discovered, was given her food after she got back from the walk. A perfect arrangement! It meant that she could then go off and have a nice doze, somewhere cool.

But she didn't understand any of that and it seemed a friendly gesture, so we started going for walks with them.

Walks are an odd occupation for a dog who has lived all his or her life in the wild. In the wild, you walk through necessity. A house dog does it to get exercise. Or maybe it's so that the humans can get exercise? Whatever the reason, I quickly grew to rather enjoy going for a walk. But Dog never did. Well, he did – but he went off chasing birds and rooting about and might just as well have been on his own. He never really bothered with the humans much on those walks and didn't come when he was called. Dog was very independent. He'd had to be.

The first walk we did, we went right past the bins where our nest had been. I actually went and sniffed the bush we'd slept under. It smelled of dog – but not of us. Someone else must have moved in.

I went to the place where you can see right down the valley. It was so long since we'd left the big water that I was beginning to forget what it felt like to splash out into the deep until you were running on nothing at all and there was only water underneath your feet.

Another evening we went down to the green valley and very close to our scrape-nest. Dog actually accompanied us on part of that walk. I think he was interested to return there himself. He and I ran off, leaving Fanny barking and complaining. We found our nest and sat in it together. After a while we heard the humans calling for us.

I was anxious that we should go back to them. I didn't want to risk annoying them. But Dog lay back and scratched himself in a relaxed way.

'Let them call, Kitty,' he told me. 'The more anxious they get about us, the more they begin to worry about us, the better. In that way we'll sort of become their dogs without them noticing. They'll start believing they own us – and then they'll have to look after us.'

Maybe he was right. I certainly didn't want to go back to them straight away – not on that occasion. It was so good being in the scrape-nest again.

'I like it here,' I said. 'It feels like a real nest!'

Dog growled. I'd been giving him a bad time about our place near the swing chairs and I suppose he was getting tired of hearing me nagging and complaining.

But I couldn't help it. Recently I'd been getting more and more desperate to have a proper nest. I imagined Dog and me living there together. But it wouldn't just be the two of us; we wouldn't be alone there. At first I couldn't under-stand who it was I wanted to share the nest with – apart from Dog. Then it had dawned on me. I was thinking it might be rather nice if our puppies were living there with us. I didn't mention this to Dog. I wasn't sure how he'd take to the idea.

'It seems ages since we were here,' I said, sniffing the grass and listening to a bird singing, high in a tree.

Dog sighed beside me and stretched out in the cool shade. 'It's good, isn't it?' he said, licking my ear so that it tickled.

'Stop it!' I complained, pulling away from him and shaking my head.

'You smell good!' Dog said and he snuggled up close to me. I could feel his hot breath panting on my neck. He smelled good as well. He smelled of all the best dog smells; of bread and biscuits and nice food; a warm, happy, safe – and at the same time a bit scary – kind of smell.

'We should go back to Joanna and David!' I yelped.

'Not yet,' he growled.

But I got up and ran away.

It's odd how sometimes you do the very thing you don't want to do. I ran away when every bit of me wanted to stay there with him in our scrape-nest, surrounded by the cool grass and the sounds and smells of the country. But I was afraid; afraid of what might happen if I stayed. I'd never known Dog seem so alive before. He wasn't racing about or anything. He was just pressed up close to me. But I could smell the life in him. I wanted to take that life and to share it with him. I wanted him to give me his life – but I didn't know what that meant. I didn't want him to die. Not that! Never, ever that! But I did want to take the life out of him and have it inside me. I wanted us, somehow, to be so joined together that no matter what happened, we'd never be apart again. I wanted to take Dog and make him into my puppies. Our puppies. Dog's and mine.

I wanted that so much and yet I ran away from him – because the idea terrified me.

Chapter Twenty-One

My longing for puppies didn't go away. In fact, over the next few days it got stronger and stronger. I think Dog understood. I think, maybe, he wanted them as well. But a new problem had now presented itself.

Or maybe I should have said 'themselves'. Other dogs! It seemed as though every dog in the village was suddenly interested in me – the house dogs of the local humans as well as the strays from miles around. They all came sniffing round the place with the swing seats, howling and barking at me.

I don't know what I thought about it. I was frightened a bit; but I was also excited. I remembered Mother telling us girls about 'the time being right to have puppies'. I supposed that my 'time' had come.

I think it was worse for Dog than it was for me. He got so jealous. He spent his time fighting off the other dogs. But he couldn't manage it single-handed and more than once one of them got hold of me. They were rough creatures and smelled hot and dangerous. I fought them off as well. I suppose they each wanted me to have their puppies. But I only wanted Dog's, you see. I didn't want just any puppies. They had to be Dog's and mine. He was the gentle one. He was the one I loved. He was the one I'd lived with all the time I'd been in the wild. It was only natural that I should want his life and that he would give it to me.

And when that did eventually happen, it wasn't frightening at all. In fact, it only made me love him more.

But even then the other dogs wouldn't go away. They wanted to share me, I think.

Eventually it got so bad that very early one morning we moved from our place near the swing seats and went all the way to The View. I suppose we hoped that the other dogs wouldn't follow us there. But they did.

I jumped down onto the ledge in the belief that I could hide from them or that at least they wouldn't be able to reach me. But that meant I was separated from Dog and I wished I hadn't as soon as I'd done it.

Gradually, one by one, the other dogs arrived up at The View. I could see their heads sticking out over the top wall, looking down at me. They howled and whined and kept fighting amongst themselves. Some of them leaned right over the wall, reaching down with their front legs, daring themselves to jump down beside me. I knew it would only be a question of time before one of them managed it – and once one had, they'd all follow.

I was really terrified by now. I could see Dog fighting them off, growling and snapping. At one point he was in the middle of a real battle. The noise was appalling.

Then David stuck his head out of the upstairs window.

He was shouting at the dogs and clapping his hands. But it didn't do any good. It just made the dogs more excited. They yelped and barked with added gusto.

Joanna appeared, down on the short grass. She was holding a hose in her hand. Out of the end came a stream of water. She aimed it up at the top of the wall and tried to squirt it at the dogs. But the water reached nowhere near them. Then she called to me: 'Kitty! Jump down! Come on . . . Kitty!' She was holding out a hand and I realized that she was trying to tempt me down into the garden.

I looked over the precipice at her. My ears flopped forward and my head was on one side. I wasn't sure even then that I could really trust her. Her face looked kind and her voice was gentle. But why now – suddenly – was I being invited into the garden? Was it a trap?

Then something happened that put a quick end to my hesitation. I heard a funny, scratching, sliding noise and, looking over my shoulder, I saw a dog slipping and falling down the wall. He was a big, mangy brown creature. He was panting heavily and as soon as his feet touched the level he made a dive for me.

I didn't wait. I launched myself off that ledge and sailed down to the ground, landing with a bump within inches of Joanna.

'David!' she shouted. 'One of them has got down onto the terrace . . .'

'Well, I can't do anything, dearest . . .'

'How will it get back? Go on! Shoo!' she shouted, taking a small pebble and throwing it up at the brown dog. He, meanwhile, was looking over the side with a puzzled expression. I expect he was one of those dogs who thought a lot about himself. He probably couldn't understand why I wasn't interested in him.

Joanna kneeled on the grass and held her hand out for me to sniff. This is a sign of friendship, coming from a human. It gives us dogs a chance to check what sort of mood the human is in. If they're up to no good, you can usually smell it on them.

Joanna smelled very sweet and a bit sleepy. I think all the noise had woken her up. Perhaps she and David had their nest in the upstairs room, I thought.

Then, as if to confirm this idea, Fanny came running out of the house and she stretched and barked, as though she'd just got up as well.

She raced over and sniffed me. Then she stood back. 'It's your time, isn't it?' she said, speaking with great authority.

'I think so,' I replied.

'You're not much more than a pup yourself,' she remarked. 'Is it your first time?' And when I told her, in a shaky voice, that it was, she ran round me, barking and snapping.

'Stop it, Fan!' Joanna told her, pushing her away. I think she thought Fanny was wanting a fight. (I've noticed with humans that they can't always tell what is a fight and what's just play.)

Then Joanna reached out and stroked me.

I know this will seem almost unbelievable, but I'd hardly ever been stroked by a human before. It was such an unusual experience that I looked up at the top of the wall – wanting Dog to see what was happening. There was a line of dogs' faces all looking down. Dog was in the middle of them. He barked, once. I'm not sure what it was he was saying.

The brown dog, meanwhile, was pacing backwards and forwards along the ledge. He found a place where he could get a footing in a crack in the back wall. From there he managed to scramble and claw his way up to the top level again and rejoin the other dogs.

'She's on heat,' David said, walking out onto the lawn and leaning over Joanna, who was still on her hands and knees, stroking me.

'Poor little thing! She's terrified.'

They were talking about me. That was another first! I was being stroked and talked about. It was almost like being a house dog.

That evening they fed me in the garden. But they took Dog's scraps and put them in the usual place outside the brown door.

'I don't know what you're up to,' Fanny said as she and the humans were going off for a walk.

'I'm not up to anything,' I replied. And, really, I was as confused as she was about what was going on.

Joanna and David took me through the iron gate and they locked it behind them. We were in the area next to the big blue water.

'We could leave her out here,' Joanna suggested.

'Dearest, if we do that,' David said, 'she's halfway to moving in!'

'Just till she's off heat,' Joanna said.

'What about Bailey?'

'He'll be all right . . .'

They sort of muttered like this all the way down the sloping track to the parked van and the brown door. I followed after them, wanting to get some idea of what they intended to do.

Then Joanna paused and looked back at me. 'We'll leave you in here, Kitty. So the other dogs won't bother you . . .' And she and David and Fanny went out into the lane.

As the door was closing, I got a glimpse of Bailey looking in.

'What should I do?' I barked.

'Stay inside,' he shouted. He sounded excited.

Then the door closed and I heard the click of a lock.

I sat down then — just where I was on the hard stone step at the bottom of the sloping track. I was all alone. The lower garden spread out, huge and unexplored to one side of me. The high wall separated me from the familiar lane. The sweet smells of different flowers and growing plants, the buzzing of insects and the gurgling of water surrounded me like a strange and heady mixture of all the nice things in the world. This is it, I told myself. I'm where I've dreamed of being. I'm inside the magic garden.

So why didn't I feel glad? It was what I'd wanted. But now that it'd happened I felt almost . . . dejected.

'Dog!' I whined. 'Dog . . .'

I'd discovered that even paradise could be lonely.

Chapter Twenty-Two

But it wasn't lonely for long.

When they came back from their walk I was still sitting where they'd left me on the bottom step of the sloping path. The brown door opened and Fanny came bustling in. But to my amazement, before Joanna and David followed her, Dog bounded past them and raced up to me barking and yelping in an over-excited way.

'Yes, all right, Bailey! All right!' David said, trying to quieten him. But Dog, when he was excited, could be unstoppable.

'Oh, Kitty!' Joanna said, bending down and stroking my head. 'Have you been waiting for us?'

Then she walked ahead of us up the path, calling; 'Come and have some water, all of you.'

She took us all, Dog included, past the blue-water pool and through the iron gates right into the top garden.

Fanny bounded ahead of her and, as soon as Joanna had unlocked the big double doors of the house, Fanny and she went inside.

I was about to follow them when Dog put a paw on my tail.

'A little at a time, Kitty!' he whispered. 'Don't be over-eager.'

We could see Joanna and Fanny in a room next to the front door. This had big window-doors and Joanna came and opened them. The smell that came from that room! I thought it must have been the place where she kept all the scraps. It smelled — well, there really isn't any possibility that I could describe it! It simply smelled of every nice taste that has ever been invented. It smelled of that most desirable thing of all — fresh food. To a dog in the wild there can be no more exciting or enchanting experience than that smell — apart from eating the stuff, of course.

As soon as she'd opened the window she went to a tap and filled a bowl with water. She was doing it for us. She brought that bowl and put it down on the ground near us.

'Bailey, you must be thirsty after the walk. Have some water. You too, Kitty!' Then, raising her voice a little, she called, 'Yes, Fan. I'll do your supper now.'

Fanny barked once and sounded a bit impatient. So after we'd both had a drink we went off and sat in the shade. We could hear Fanny wolfing down her supper in the food room.

Apparently Dog had decided to go on the walk that evening. Apparently he'd made himself adorable to Joanna and David. Apparently it was all part of his plan.

But actually I suspected that it was Fanny who got permission for him to stay inside the garden with me. Dog was very attractive and although Fanny was older than us, I'd noticed the way she looked at him. I remember thinking even then that I'd have to be on my guard. Dog was so polite he'd be bound to let Fanny flirt with him. But if she tried anything on with him, she'd soon find out that I could be a mean fighter and she might live to regret it.

We slept that night in a nest we dug down in a corner of the lower garden. David took us out there late in the evening. He went down to the brown door and we remained sitting halfway up the sloping path, watching him. We both thought that maybe he was going to make us leave the garden. But instead he locked the brown door with us on the inside. We were so relieved. Then he came back up the path.

It was quite dark by then. We reached the blue-water pool. Its surface glimmered and wrinkled like silk, twinkling and flashing in the pale light of the moon.

'All right, you two,' he said, 'You can spend tonight out here. Then the dogs won't bother Kitty.' And he gave us each a crunchy little biscuit that tasted of meat. We had to take them straight from his fingers. I grabbed mine and ran away. But Dog was braver. That very first time he actually licked David's hand – or so he claims.

'Why?' I asked him, when he told me.

'I was saying thank you,' he replied.

David went in through the iron gates and closed them after him. 'Goodnight, Kitty! Goodnight, Bailey!' he called, disappearing into the dark along the narrow path that led between high hedges all the way to the front door.

I have a picture in my mind from that evening. Dog is sitting with his back to me, his nose pressed between the bars of the iron gate, watching David's shadow disappearing into the gloom. I can see Dog's white fur glowing in the moonlight and his eager, tense, trembling body.

He didn't say anything. He didn't need to. I think we both knew we'd come home at last.

Chapter Twenty-Three

And that's where we remained for quite some time. Joanna and David seemed to get used to us having a nest in the corner of what we learned to call the vegetable garden. During the day we were allowed into the top garden and the three of us – Fanny, Dog and I – would play together, chasing through the bushes and exploring.

There was garden right round the house and the areas were quite different from each other. There was one place where Joanna hung up big squares of material and clothes that humans wear on a long line of string. The things were always wet when she put them on the line and the first time it happened they dripped on me. She put them there to get dry, of course, just like we used to let the sun dry us after we'd been into the big water.

Joanna and David used to sit under the porch in front of the doors in the middle of the morning with a hot brown drink that smelled of burned seeds. Then in the middle of the day they had food at a long table in the shade of the trees on the short grass near the high wall with The View at its top. They used the blue-water pool to 'swim' in. That's what they called it when the land isn't under your feet any more and you're surrounded by water. Later in the day they'd go up to the room with the balcony and Fanny would go with them. They'd have a sleep, I think, just as Dog and I did in the afternoon. Then they'd come down and have another hot drink. This one smelled of grass and sweet herbs. Then we'd all go out for a walk before coming home and being fed. Fanny had her supper in the kitchen and we had our scraps in the garden. Much later in the evening, when it was getting dark, Joanna and David would have more to eat. They had this food at the long table under the trees. They would put flickering flame lights on the table and I used to watch the moths flying into the yellow. Sometimes, however, they had this meal – their 'supper' – in a room of the house. This room was on the other side of the front door from the food room. It also had long window-doors and we could see a table and chairs in it.

All that we knew about the inside of the house was what we saw through these windows. We never went in ourselves. Not then. That was Fanny's place. And if I dared to set so much as a paw inside the front doors she would come bounding out, barking and snarling and making a terrible fuss.

'Come away, Kitty!' Dog would snap. 'That's Fanny's nest.'

'I was only looking,' I'd protest.

That was our life, really; our life in the magic garden. Sleeping in our nest, playing in the garden, going for a walk and waiting to be fed.

Joanna and David did a lot of other things as well – but they didn't really concern us and some were a bit hard to understand. Every morning David poked about in the blue-water pool – 'cleaning' it, he said. And he dug in the vegetable garden and poured water on the plants. Joanna did the same to the flowers in the upper garden and she went to the shop in the village most days. David went for the post each morning. He got it from the counter place where we'd first seen him. He'd let Dog and me go with him if we wanted to and sometimes Fanny came too. David also did things with a funny little box. Sometimes he held it to his eye and at other times he stood it on three long, thin legs. He would then point it at people or, quite often, at us. There'd be a funny, buzzing click sound. The first time it happened I thought it might be a kind of gun – like the one the man had down in the big valley. I shot away out of sight and hid for ages under a hedge.

'Come on, Kitty!' he called, using his most persuasive voice. 'Come on! Let me take your picture!'

I had no idea what he was talking about and I stayed well out of his way.

But even picture-taking I got used to in time. He was always doing it. It got to be quite ordinary.

Life became a routine. We soon knew what we'd be doing most hours of the day. There was a set pattern to our existence and, if I'm honest, it sometimes got a bit boring in the early days. I'd been so used to excitement and danger that I found it almost hard to settle down to being safe and knowing that I was going to be fed without having to go searching for scraps.

Now, if *I* was feeling that, then how much more dull must it have seemed to Dog? But if it was, then never once did he say so. I think he valued our safety much more than I did. I think he realized how close we had got to starving when we were out in the wild. Remember, he had lived longer than me. He'd seen each of the seasons. He knew how many dangers lay waiting ahead for us. For this reason I think he was prepared to put up with a bit of boredom. I think he almost welcomed it.

Besides, Dog wasn't the type to ever be bored for long. He always found some adventure to keep him occupied. Early on he found a way in and out of the vegetable garden without having to wait for the humans to open the brown door. He discovered a place where he could climb up a mound of earth and from it jump onto the top of the side wall. He then ran along the top of this wall to a place where he could jump down onto some scrubby grass and thorns. Then, by wriggling under some wire netting and going along the side of a dusty patch of soil, he could reach the road outside the village, not far from the track that led down to the green valley and our scrape-nest.

I went with him a few times in the early days but I didn't like the thorns much, and anyway I was beginning to enjoy a life of leisure. So usually I let him go off on his own.

Sometimes Dog would be gone all day. But he always came back in time for supper. No matter how far he'd been, no matter what adventures he'd had, he was always there, panting and excited, by the time we came back from our walk. I don't think Joanna and David had any idea what he was doing – not in the early days. I think they believed he'd been with me all the time and that, when we all returned from a walk, he'd been with us every step of the way.

Not that Joanna and David's lives were a set routine. They had a lot of other humans who came to the house.

These people would stay for a while and then they'd disappear. One day they'd be there, the next they'd have gone — and it would be almost as though we'd never seen them. I found this a bit hard to get used to. Particularly as there were so many different varieties of human. It could get confusing. Not only did their shapes differ — as indeed dogs' shapes differ — but their behaviour was so variable. Most were friendly towards us; but they had such different ways of showing this friendship. Some wanted to stroke us, others wanted to throw things and play games. One or two were really generous about slipping us bits of food when Joanna and David weren't looking. Then there were a few who seemed hardly to notice that we existed.

Once, when I was having a doze on the grass, a large fat man nearly sat on me. He threw himself down on top of me and I only just escaped being squashed to death. Even when I leaped free, he didn't notice me. I think he'd had too much red liquid with his lunch. That did happen sometimes. The humans who came were called 'guests' — they all had this name. Joanna and David would give the guests lunch at the table in the garden. Most of them drank this liquid — what David called 'wine'. Some guests, like the fat man, were inclined to drink too much of it. It made them noisy and stupid. As I say, I was nearly crushed to death by him and afterwards he just fell fast asleep on the grass, and snored very loudly.

Fanny gradually got accustomed to our being there. She liked Dog more than me and she didn't pretend otherwise. 'Bailey,' she'd say, 'would you like to share this scrap with me?' Or, 'Bailey, shall we go and look at the blue-water pool?' And Dog would wag his tail and scamper off after her. It made me sick!

One night as we were settling down in the vegetable garden he said, in a half-sleepy voice, 'You'll have to get inside before the winter comes.'

'Inside where?' I growled. I hated it when he started this sort of conversation just when we were going off to sleep. If it got worrying, it could keep me awake for hours.

'Inside the house.'

'Why?'

'Well, we want the puppies to be house dogs, don't we?'

I sat up then and looked at him. This was really serious. 'What puppies?' I asked.

'Yours and mine.'

'Are we having some?' I gasped.

'Haven't you noticed?' he said.

'Noticed?'

'You've put on weight, Kitty.'

'I wish you wouldn't call me that stupid name,' I yelped.

'It's about time you called me Bailey,' he growled.

'You're not Bailey. You're Dog. You're Dog and I'm Little,' I snapped. And I got up and moved away from the nest out into the cool, dark garden.

'Not if we're house dogs . . .'

'We're not house dogs. We're us,' I barked. 'I don't know what's got into you, Dog. I don't honestly.' I could feel hot tears stinging my eyes and my voice started to tremble.

'I know what's the matter with you,' he said. 'I've seen it before.' He made it sound deep and mysterious.

I think Dog had a whole other life before he met me. I think he got up to all sorts of pranks. I dare say he'd been a bit of a lad. I dare say there were litters of Dog's puppies the length and breadth of the big valley.

The very idea made me furious!

'If you're going to talk nonsense, I shall sleep elsewhere,' I whined.

'You wait,' Dog said and he sighed contentedly.

I thought he'd come and get me. I thought he'd wheedle and flatter me and persuade me back to the nest. But he didn't. I could hear his breathing getting longer and deeper. He was going to sleep.

'You can't sleep now!' I barked.

'What?' he grunted, waking with a start.

'You can't sleep now! How do you know I'm going to have puppies?'

'Because your tummy is swelling.'

It was true that it was a bit bigger but I thought it was because we'd been getting regular food. I thought I was just putting on weight. I didn't know I had puppies growing inside me.

'Oh, Dog!' I said. Then, when he still remained silent, I crept back to the nest and slipped in beside him. I was suddenly afraid. I wanted him to reassure me. 'Bailey,' I whispered.

He turned then and licked my ear.

'Are you sure?' I asked him.

'Not completely – but almost sure.'

'You don't mind?'

'Little!' he whispered.

He could be so complex. He could be so unexpected. But he could also be so wise.

I knew he was right this time.

'We're going to have puppies,' I whispered.

'No. Not us, you! You're going to have them, Kitty!'

'But they will be ours,' I told him. 'Yours and mine.'

'Go to sleep, Little,' he said quietly. 'You'll need a lot of rest.'

'I like it best when you call me Little,' I murmured.

Chapter Twenty-Four

A day or two later I decided to tell Fanny my news. Once I realized what was happening to me it seemed natural to confide in her.

We were lying in the shade of the porch. Dog had gone off on one of his wanders and Joanna and David were both busy. So we had the place to ourselves.

'Do you know anything about puppies?' I asked her, trying to keep my voice ordinary and stop it trembling.

'Of course I do,' she replied, using an irritatingly superior tone.

'I thought you would,' I said, yawning and feigning indifference.

'Well, I would, wouldn't I?' she said.

'Not necessarily,' I muttered. 'I don't know much myself.'

'That's because you've never had any.'

'Of course I haven't!' I said. The idea seemed almost shocking.

'But I have, you see,' Fanny said, bending and licking her tummy.

'You have?' I yelped. She certainly was full of surprises.

'Yes.'

'When?'

'Ages ago.'

'You've never told me before.'

'I don't talk about it,' she replied.

'Where are they?' I asked. I looked around. I think I was half expecting to see them.

'Gone,' Fanny growled.

'Gone? Where? Did they run off?'

'House puppies don't run off. They're not strays, you know.'

Fanny has always managed to make the word 'stray' sound inferior. I think she does it to remind me that I'm one. I suppose I always will be in her eyes. No matter how much Joanna and David look after me, I'll always be the stray they took in.

'If they don't run off, what happens to them?'

'They get given away to other humans.'

This seemed to me the most peculiar idea. It didn't make sense.

'But why?' I demanded.

'Humans only ever want one house dog,' Fanny replied with that 'surely you know that' tone of voice.

'But – what about Dog and me?' I said. I hope I made it sound as though I was scoring a point. I wanted to show that I thought Fanny was talking nonsense.

Her next words, therefore, cut right through me.

'They're not going to keep you, Kitty. You surely didn't think that?'

'Not keep us?' I was shattered by the suggestion. 'You mean they're going to send us back to the wild?'

'No! They like you and they'd worry about you in the wild. No. They're looking for other humans who want a house dog. Then they'll give you away.'

I think there was a bit of a silence then. I think I actually saw all our happiness, Dog's and mine, breaking up into little pieces — as sunlight does when it shines on the surface of the blue-water pool.

'Oh, Fanny!' I whispered.

She looked down over the edge of the wicker armchair. She had her head on one side and her eyes — which are big and, I must admit, rather beautiful — actually looked troubled.

'I'm sorry,' she mumbled. 'I thought you knew.'

'No. I thought they liked us . . .'

'They do. They do, Kitty. But they've already got me . . .'

'You don't want us? Is that it?'

'No! If I'm honest, I quite like having you here. And darling Bailey is great fun!'

She added the bit about 'darling Bailey' with disgusting enthusiasm, I thought.

'But if humans only want one house dog,' I whined, 'then no one will want to take Bailey and me — because we're two.'

'You're two, yes,' Fanny agreed and maybe I chose not to notice her mournful voice.

'So they won't be able to give us away!' I felt instantly relieved.

But Fanny looked gloomy and soon changed my mood.

'I'm afraid you'll be separated, Kitty. You'll both be sent to live in different places. You could be miles apart. The world is very large. Some of the guests have to fly to get here.'

It took a moment for her words to sink in. She had just suggested the most unthinkable possibility. Was she really saying that Dog and I would be separated because we'd found our way into the magic garden? Was that to be our reward, after we'd worked so hard to get here? No! It couldn't happen. It would be too cruel.

'What can we do?' I gasped. My whole life was suddenly under threat and yet the day had started just like any other. We were both lying comfortably in the cool of the porch and I had thought to tell Fanny my great news about the puppies.

'What about them?' I added, speaking my thoughts out loud.

'About who?'

'My puppies?' I whimpered.

'Oh, don't even think about having puppies!' Fanny told me, completely unaware that I was already carrying them in my tummy. 'Your human will decide when you're going to have puppies. You need to get settled first . . .'

I waited until that evening to tell Dog. But before I had a chance to begin, he started talking. He was full of news. Apparently he'd made friends with another human in the village. This man had a garden place a little way out in the country – an easy walk away. He called this place a 'campo' and grew vegetables there, I think. The man evidently liked Dog very much and used to look out for him and take him with him to the campo when he went there. What was more important was that Dog liked him. They'd been spending hours together – whole days sometimes. Dog hadn't told me before because he wasn't sure that the friendship would last. But that very day the man, who Dog said was called 'Mel', had brought a wooden box to his campo and put it under a bush. It was for Dog to use – as a sort of nest.

'It's like being a house dog in the wild, Kitty . . . And he brings me scraps.'

'You like it better than here?' I asked him. Then I didn't listen to his answer. I was deep in my own thoughts, while Dog's voice chattered on, giving me all the exciting details of his new life.

I discovered that evening how alone you can be. I had this terrible piece of news to tell and yet Dog was full of other stories. He was so happy and so excited and so . . . alive. I didn't want to spoil it for him. I couldn't have borne watching his face turn worried and disappointed. So I decided to wait till another occasion. I decided to say nothing.

Maybe, I thought, we could escape from the magic garden and we could both go and live with Mel. We'd both be 'house dogs in the wild'. But what about my puppies? This 'Mel' would never feed all my puppies and look after them. Not like Joanna would. If we were going to have puppies, I wanted them here, in the magic garden, with Joanna and David. I wanted them to be safe. I wanted them to be house puppies. I've seen what happens to wild puppies. They join gangs and get more and more fierce. They fight amongst themselves. They get ill and limp and starve. The wild is no life for a puppy. Nor would it be good for me in my present condition. I needed good regular food to give me the strength to feed the puppies. Dog himself had told me that. You don't get strength in the wild. I remembered how thin and tired we'd grown. I remembered how I'd nearly died. I couldn't let that happen to me again. Not now I was going to be a mother. 'Mel' might bring scraps, but we needed proper food, my puppies and I. Joanna's food. And now, when everything had seemed to be working out for us, it was all going wrong. And only I knew. I was alone with my knowledge. While all the time Dog was chattering on – so excited about the new prospects, so glad to be alive.

'You want to go and live with this Mel, don't you? You want to leave me,' I howled. I couldn't stop shaking. I sobbed and sobbed, pulling away from him and not letting him comfort me. In the end he became quite concerned about me.

'Whatever is wrong, Little?' he said. 'Of course I don't want to live with him. I like visiting him, that's all. This is home. You know that. This is our base. From here we can have all the adventures we want. You'll be a house dog, with your puppies. And I'll be . . . a half house dog.' He rolled over and scratched his back on the rough earth. Then he sighed. 'It couldn't be better! We've got everything we need – well, we will have once we've got you inside the house. Once you're in and safe I'll be able to go off from time to time . . .'

'Off?' I said. I hardly needed to ask the next question. I already knew what he was thinking.

'I do still want to go to the high mountains, Little,' he murmured. And his eyes took on that faraway look that I hadn't seen for so long. 'I haven't forgotten, or given up my dream,' he continued – he sounded almost apologetic. 'I'm sorry, I thought you'd know that . . .'

'Know?' I gasped, unable to stop my voice trembling.

'I still want to see the snow,' he whispered.

How could I tell him then that our carefully worked-out life was in danger of collapsing? How could I tell him that there was even the possibility that he and I could be separated; that we might be sent away to be house dogs far away from each other? How could I tell him, when he was so full of excitement? How could I spoil his dream? I hadn't the heart.

So I kept silent that night and later, while he lay sleeping beside me, sometimes grunting and squeaking at one of his sleep-dreams, I wished with all the power in my body and the thoughts in my head that something would come along to help us. I didn't very often wish things for myself – and really this time I was wishing for Dog as well, for both of us. And I was wishing for our puppies; for our family.

'I wish something would happen to make Joanna and David have to keep us,' I whispered. 'I wish there was something I could do that would stop them thinking of us as strays. I wish they would want us to belong to them . . .'

I don't think I slept much that night – I was wishing so hard. I wished on all the lonely stars in the sky. I even wished on Dog and myself.

'Just let them want to keep us,' I pleaded to the empty night. 'I can bear anything, if only they'll keep us.'

Chapter Twenty-Five

The very next day (perhaps in answer to my wish) a new guest arrived. He was a tall, quietly spoken, gentle man and I liked him at once.

Joanna and David seemed very pleased that he was there and I thought that while they were enjoying themselves with him they wouldn't be bothering about what to do with Dog and me. So I tried not to think about our future. I even made myself stop worrying about the puppies. After all, it was still early days, I told myself. I wasn't entirely sure how long it took to have puppies (that was one of the things I'd meant to ask Fanny) but while there were no real signs that I was carrying them, I thought I'd be pretty safe. The fact that Dog had noticed was because . . . well, he looked at me more than any other creature ever did – or, I think, ever will. At that time even Fanny was still unaware – and I reckoned that Fanny would be the first to know, particularly as she'd had puppies of her own. When Fanny noticed what was happening to me – then I'd do something about it. (What? That was one of the things I was trying not to worry about.)

On the third day of the new guest's visit, they all went off in the van together. Fanny often went in the van. She usually told me all about it when she came back. She sometimes went to a town – which I later discovered is only a very big village and is horribly busy and noisy, although she made it sound very grand and special. On other occasions she went for what were called 'trips'. Trips were longer and sometimes they'd be away all day. I didn't mind. Although David always locked the metal gate of the top garden when they went out, he sometimes left me inside. Besides, by then both Dog and I had discovered a way out of that garden into the vegetable garden, so really we were free to come and go as we chose. Dog was very keen on the idea of these trips. 'On a trip,' he told me, 'we could go all the way to the high mountains and back. I'd really like to go on a trip, Kitty.' (He was calling me Kitty all the time again. I think he thought that if he did, then somehow it would help to get me inside the house.)

But this new guest, whose name was Bryn, wanted me to get in the car with them.

'No!' Joanna exclaimed. 'Kitty doesn't come with us!'

'Why not?' Bryn asked. He seemed quite upset that I was being left behind. 'I expect you'd love to come, wouldn't you?' he said, bending down and stroking behind my ear.

I licked his hand, wagged my tail and didn't go with them, of course. But he had wanted me to – that was what seemed important. Bryn had automatically treated me like a house dog. Maybe he didn't know that I was a stray? Or maybe he knew and he just didn't mind. Whatever the reason, he did seem to think of me as part of the household.

That evening, over supper at the long table, Bryn talked about nothing else. By then, of course, I was seriously listening to everything the humans said. I didn't want to miss a single word. After all, it might have been our future that was being discussed. I hoped Dog would listen as well. That would have been a good way for him to discover how uncertain the future was looking for us. For some reason I dreaded having to tell him. I suppose I didn't want to be the bearer of bad news. But Dog had been chasing birds most of the day up at Mel's campo and he was fast asleep the whole time and didn't hear any of what was said.

David explained that he was worried about having three dogs to look after. And Joanna added that it'd be impossible when they needed to go away. Fanny was easy to deal with, she explained. They either took her with them in the car – 'Then take the other two as well!' Bryn cried – or, if they were 'going abroad' (which I think meant 'flying'), there were other people who were used to taking her and looking after her until they returned.

Fanny confirmed this later. Apparently at least once a year Joanna and David went away and left her behind. Sometimes she went to stay with other humans. When I asked about this, she became strangely silent and wouldn't say anything more about it. I wanted to know where she went and who these other humans were, but she quickly changed the subject. She told me that at other times a human came and stayed in the house in the magic garden and looked after her there. She didn't mind talking about that. But she wouldn't talk about where she went to stay, away from the house. I didn't know why. Fanny used to be such a puzzle. She was so full of secret bits. But, at the time. I had my own life to sort out and couldn't be side-tracked by thinking about her. From what she said, it seemed to me that everything was very well organized by Joanna and David. I agreed with Bryn. I couldn't see why there was a problem. If it was all right for Fanny to be 'looked after,' then Dog and I could be looked after also. We'd fit in. After all, we'd been doing precisely that ever since we'd arrived.

The following day Bryn was playing with me on the cut grass. He liked lying down beside me and stroking me and tickling my tummy and behind my ears. I let him, because I thought it made him happy. This time, however, he kept whispering to me as well.

'It's all right, Kitty,' he said. 'I'll look after you. I won't let them send you away.'

Actually this was the first time anyone apart from Fanny had ever admitted in my hearing that we were going to be 'sent away'. It made my heart stop, just to hear him say the words. Also I wasn't at all sure that he would be able to persuade them differently. I mean, he didn't live in the magic garden so it wasn't really any concern of his.

Then Joanna came out of the food room and caught him whispering to me. 'Look at you two!' she called. 'You be a good girl, Kitty, and Bryn will pop you in his case and take you home with him.'

I wriggled away from Bryn. I was shaking so violently that I could hardly stand. I was being trapped!

'Kitty!' he called. 'What's the matter? Come on . . .' And he crawled towards me over the grass, holding his hand out and beckoning to me.

He wants to take me, I thought. That's what all this is about. It's going to happen now. He'll take me now, while Dog is away at the stupid campo with Mel. Dog will come back tonight and I won't be here.

Fanny came out of the house, yawning and stretching. 'Mmmh!' she growled. 'You've got yourself a new friend, I see.'

That did it. She was confirming everything I suspected. Bryn had come to take me away with him, back to his home. The whole thing was a trap.

I turned tail and fled out of the garden.

I ran past the blue-water pool and down the sloping track. David was watering plants in the vegetable garden. As I raced past, he looked up and called, 'Where are you off to?'

I didn't pause to answer. I made for our nest corner and then climbed the pile of earth. I jumped onto the wall and ran, balancing precariously, to the end. Then I dropped down onto the thorn patch. By now Dog had made quite a track with all his comings and goings and it was easy for me to find the way under the wire netting and along the side of the dusty field. Eventually, breathless and shaking, I came out onto the road.

Only then did I rest. Only then did I realize that I didn't know where I was going. My one thought had been to find Dog and warn him of what was happening. But I didn't know where he was. Almost certainly he'd be at the campo with Mel. But he'd never told me its whereabouts. Or, if he had, then I hadn't listened.

I hadn't listened! I'd been so bound up with my own worries that I hadn't listened to Dog.

'Dog!' I barked. 'Dog! Dog!'

The dog that lives in the counter place came running up the road, wanting to know what was happening. He sniffed me. But I didn't want to bother with him.

'Dog!' I barked.

'Which dog?' the counter-place dog asked. 'Will any dog do?'

'Go away,' I growled. I must have sounded quite fierce, I think, because his tail went down and he wandered off as though he had something else that he needed to be getting on with.

I turned away and ran a few paces up the road. I went to the edge and looked out over the valley. 'Dog!' I shouted. *Dog! Dog! Dog!* my voice echoed back at me from the distant hillside. But only *my* voice – never his.

It was almost midday. The sun was high in the sky. The heat was immense. It could be hours before Dog returned and when he did I might miss him. There were several ways that he could approach his secret path into the garden. I thought I should probably go and wait by the wall. But I felt faint with fear.

This is a scrape I'm in, I thought and I knew at once what I had to do.

I ran back to the track by the human building. It was the way down to the green valley. There was water down there – and I was very thirsty. But I don't know why I felt so shaky. Even the land seemed to be moving up and down under my paws. It was more like the big water than the solid earth.

I staggered and slipped and crawled down that hot, dusty path. When I reached the shade of the first trees I lay down in the cool to rest before I could go any further.

There was such a pain in my tummy and the inside of my head throbbed and felt horribly hot.

But mainly I had such a terrible thirst. It was this need for water that dragged me back up onto my feet. I continued to move down the narrow winding path. The grasses on either side were brown and withered; the land was parched.

When I reached the spring, the water was reduced to a trickle. I lapped from the pool and once I was refreshed I searched for our scrape-nest.

The raised earth that we had dug into a shallow hollow was mostly flattened now and the bush overhead looked dusty and dry. But I flopped down under it and after digging about a little, to level the surface of the ground and make it more comfortable to lie on, I let the heavy, swooning heat close my eyes and I passed into a strange, restless sleep.

Chapter Twenty-six

I've asked Fanny to tell the next bit, because what happened that day without me being there is so important to this story that it must be told by someone who actually saw it happening.

It was quite a to-do really and I found it more than a bit bothersome. Also I'm not sure that I can remember it too clearly — it all happened simply ages ago. However, I'll try.

The morning passed quietly enough. Bryn liked swimming and went in the pool quite often. He also liked lying in the sun. So he was in and out of the water and the splashes he made were the only sounds that disturbed me as I lay dozing on my chair in the porch.

Then David came up from the vegetable garden. 'Dearest!' he called. 'Have you seen Kitty?'

Dearest is what David sometimes calls Joanna. She was in the kitchen at the time, making lunch. David went in there and I could clearly hear them talking from where I was lying.

'She was on the lawn earlier,' Joanna said. 'Actually, I think something must have upset her. She suddenly raced away. I thought she came down to you.'

'She did. But I don't know where she's gone.'

'She's probably dug a nest for herself. It's so hot . . .'

*And it was. So hot that even Bryn came back from the pool
and sat on a deckchair in the shade.*

*That was all that happened then. It wasn't until early evening
that Bailey set up the alarm.*

I remember him suddenly being there, beside me in the
scrape-nest. He seemed very agitated. He was licking the
inside of my ear and making little squeaking sounds.

I wanted to ask him what was wrong. But I couldn't
make words. My head was so full of fire and there was this
awful pain in my tummy. I tried to sit up. But I had no
strength. When I tried, I just flopped down again and then
I couldn't move at all.

Dog barked at me a few times. I think he was trying
to get me to move. Then he took hold of one of my front
paws in his mouth and tried to pull me along.

I raised my other paw then and pushed him away. I
wanted to be left alone. I could still hear him barking. But
the sounds started to echo – like the sound of barking echoes
across the valleys, bouncing from hill to hill. I closed my
ears to the sound. I just wanted to be left to go back to
sleep.

The heat was incredible. I felt as though I was on fire.
Even my sleep-dreams were hot. There were birds circling
round over my head with their wings burning brightly
against the blue sky and all the trees were aflame.

*I heard Bailey barking when he was still outside the garden.
I got down off my chair and trotted to the iron gate, to see what
was happening.*

*I got there just as he arrived, coming up from the vegetable
garden.*

142

'Now what's the matter?' I asked him. Strays can get very overexcited. But Bailey was usually so calm. I mean, he could be playful – but this barking wasn't like that. He sounded . . . desperate is the best word, I think.

'It's Kitty!' he barked as he shot past me. He chased along the path between the high hedges.

Joanna, David and Bryn were having a cup of tea under the jacaranda tree.

'Bales! What's the matter?' David asked.

'Bailey, be quiet!' Joanna said.

'There's something wrong!' Bryn exclaimed.

I'd come onto the lawn via the side entrance near the iron gates. I think I felt worried just before Bryn spoke. I knew he was right. There was something amiss.

'What is it, Bailey?' I barked.

'It's Kitty!' he yelped. 'You've got to get them to help me, Fanny. It's Kitty. I think she's . . . dying.'

'Dying?' I barked.

We were both barking now. Bailey was jumping up and down in front of David. He was in a dreadful state. He wasn't just barking. He was howling and yelping and growling. It upset me just to hear him. I started barking at Joanna and running round her feet. Bailey turned and raced up the lawn towards the side entrance . . . then he raced back and barked at David. He did this a few times.

'He wants me,' David said. His voice sounded terribly grim.

'Where's Kitty?' Joanna asked.

Bailey yelped and howled at the sound of her name.

'It's Kitty, David!' Joanna said, starting to run towards the iron gates. 'Something's happened to Kitty!'

They all started to move at once, but in different directions. I followed Joanna.

David yelled that he'd have to get his keys and he darted into the house. Bryn was pulling on a shirt and trousers and then he ran into the house to collect his shoes.

Joanna and I were halfway down to the vegetable garden by the time Bailey was at the brown gate, leaping up and down as though he longed to open the door himself.

'David,' Joanna called. 'He wants us to go outside . . .'

'I'm coming!' David shouted, and he was. He and Bryn appeared up by the pool, running down the path. I don't think David stopped to lock the iron gate, so he must have been really worried. But he did remember to lock the brown door after him. Otherwise anyone could have walked in.

Bailey raced on ahead. Then he'd skid round and chase back to be sure we were all following. I have to admit it was all a bit fast for me. It was still boiling hot and I'm not too keen on running in the heat.

We went skidding down the path that David calls the Teahouse Walk. (I don't know why he does. I never will know.) David was in the lead by now and Bryn was just after him. Joanna and I were a little way behind.

'Oh, Fanny!' Joanna sobbed. 'Please don't let anything have happened to Kitty!'

That's when I knew that Kitty and Bailey would be staying with us for ever, I think. And I have to admit that I didn't want anything to have happened to her either. I knew, if it had, that it would hurt Bailey more than he could bear, and I didn't want that for Bailey. I know about those hurts.

My steps grew slower with a sort of dread, really. I didn't want anything to have happened to Kitty, I didn't want Bailey to be hurt and, oh! I really didn't want to remember that other walk when the dreadful thing happened to my Boris.

I heard Dog barking again. But I wasn't sure if it was a sleep-dream or real. Then David was there. He lifted me up.

David is a big man but he can be very gentle. I remember him holding me in his outstretched arms.

'What's happened?' I heard Joanna say.

'I don't know!' David replied.

He sounded so worried, I wanted to comfort him. I think I licked his arm.

'She's very hot,' he said. 'But she's breathing . . .'

'We must get her to the vet,' Joanna said.

I knew what that meant. I've been to Vet lots of times. Strays don't go to Vet. It was another sign. I tried to tell Bailey. But he was in too much of a state to listen. He walked at David's feet all the way back to the village. I don't think he wanted to leave Kitty, that was why.

I tell her sometimes how lucky she is to have known that sort of love. I think it's probably one of the good things about being a stray. Dogs must form close attachments, being in the wild – because they haven't humans to look after them. Anyway, that day I really saw how much Bailey loved Kitty. I could almost have been jealous, if I hadn't been so worried for them and so horribly hot myself.

When we got back to the house Joanna brought some water for us all to drink, while David was getting the van out of the brown gate. They were going to leave Bailey and me behind with Bryn. But Bailey made such a fuss, barking and growling, that in the end we all got in.

It must have been the first time either Bailey or Kitty had been in a van. Bailey sat on the back seat, next to Joanna, with his nose pressed to the window. He was trembling all the time. Joanna had Kitty on her knee and I was on the other side of the seat, beside her. Bryn sat in front, next to David. David always drives. I don't know why. If I were a human I'd definitely drive. It's best, I think.

You have to go right over the mountain as far as the town to get to Vet. They're quite nice when you get there.

Bailey, Bryn and I stayed in the van. We had to wait ages. When David and Joanna came back they hadn't got Kitty with them.

I shut my eyes then. I didn't want to hear that something bad had happened to Kitty. I could hear Bailey whimpering. It was such a sad sound. I started to tremble as well.

'It's all right, Bailey,' Joanna said, taking him and cuddling him. 'Kitty's all right. She has to stay with the vet. But she'll be coming home. It's all right, Bailey . . .' And she started to cry. She kissed Bailey on the head, over and over again — and she cried.

It made me feel very sad, just to hear her. I licked her arm, to comfort her, and she cuddled me as well.

Chapter Twenty-Seven

I don't suppose I'll ever know exactly what happened to me. Bailey used to say that we didn't need to know. He said that was where humans came in useful. They were there to understand that sort of thing for us.

But for whatever reason, I lost my puppies. Or rather, I never had them. I was certainly going to. I had got them inside me. But something went wrong and it made me ill and because of that, in the end, they weren't able to be 'born'.

At the time it seemed the saddest thing that could possibly happen to me. But of course there were other sad things as well. Bailey said that if we'd still been living in the wild I would have died. He said that would have been much worse. He said he could live without puppies that he'd never even known, but that he wouldn't like to live without me, because he'd got used to me and I was half of his life.

He said some wonderful things to me, Bailey. I do hope I was half as loving to him and that he realized it — how much he meant to me, I mean. It seems so important to me now that he should have known that.

I stayed at Vet for several days. But Joanna and David came to see me, so I knew it was all right to be there.

Anyway, I was so weak and sleepy all the time that I scarcely knew where I was.

Then one morning they came and collected me. David carried me to the van and Joanna got in and he put me down on her lap. I was still a bit dozy but I do remember thinking: I'm going in a van for the first time in my life. Because, you see, I didn't remember the earlier time, when they'd rushed me to Vet.

When we got back to the village, David drove up the bumpy, narrow lane and round the two sharp, angled corners all the way to the brown door. I was awake by then and I recognized it all. I wondered where Bailey would be and if he was waiting anxiously for me to arrive.

Now that's an odd thing; because I did wonder where 'Bailey' was. Not 'Dog'. I think maybe being a house dog is a condition that steals over you while you're bothering about something else.

Well, I didn't have to wonder for long. He came racing down the steep path from the blue-water pool the moment Joanna got inside the brown door.

'Gently, Bailey,' she said. 'Kitty has to get better.'

But he already knew that. He was only barking because he was glad I was home.

Home! I was thinking of the place as home now. Dogs in the wild don't have homes. They have nests. It seemed almost as though I'd become a different dog while I'd been staying at Vet's. And I had, of course, in a way. Because that's when I became Kitty in my own mind. I'd left Little behind at Vet's.

Perhaps Little stayed there on purpose. Maybe she had gone with her dead puppies and was looking after them. Maybe she was being a mother to them wherever it is you go after you leave this life. I don't know! I dare say that sounds a bit silly and not real, but the idea comforted me at the time and it often has done since – so I had to say it here.

Joanna had made a special 'bed' for me in the 'dining room'. A bed is what a house dog calls her nest, and the dining room is what Joanna and David call the table room with the window-doors on the other side of the hall from the 'kitchen' (Joanna and David's name for the food room). They even let Bailey come inside the house to see me. They were being so kind.

Bryn was still there. I think he thought that it was something he'd said that had made me ill. It's a pity that we can't tell humans what we're thinking. I would like to have explained to him what it was that had upset me so. Because, of course, I'd got it all wrong. He wasn't going to take me home with him. I know that now. He's one of those guests that have to fly to get here. And I've never yet heard of a dog that flies. When he went home he made a special point of saying goodbye to me and to Bailey. I think he liked us both equally. He was a very nice human.

It was a slow process, 'getting better', and several times I had to go back to Vet. But more importantly a new life was starting for Bailey and me and it was happening almost without us knowing it. While everyone was worrying about me getting better, they were getting more and more used to having me in the house. Maybe Joanna and David thought it was only going to be temporary to begin with. But I think Fanny always knew that I'd moved in and that it was going to be a permanent arrangement.

I slept each evening in the dining room and Bailey slept in my basket on the porch. When I was a little stronger I was able to go to the window-doors and see him outside in the moonlit garden. As time passed I did begin to hope that Joanna and David would let him sleep in the dining room with me – but when I mentioned this to him he took on a rather alarmed expression.

'I don't think I'd like that, Kitty,' he explained. 'I should feel a bit trapped, you see – locked inside a human house.'

Looking back I know he was right. Bailey was only ever meant to be a half house dog. Though he was more than happy to come exploring inside during the day.

The house was really interesting. At the end of the hall there is an open space. By open I mean the sky is over-head; there isn't any roof on it. There is a room on each side of this space and on the back wall there is a door that leads out of this 'courtyard' to the narrow garden near the clothesline. There is also a small room beside the back door where Joanna keeps a lot of food in a cold box. And on the back wall of the courtyard – on the other corner from the back door – there are 'steps' that lead to the upper floor of the house.

I can't begin to explain how exciting I thought steps were the first time I went up them. It is such a brilliant way of getting up a steep cliff. Far, far easier than having to scramble. At the top of these steps there is a passage that goes round three sides of the open area. You can look down through big square windows on to the floor of the courtyard (it has a raised bit in the middle, with plants growing in it) or, when you look up, you are closer to the open sky and can see the edge of the roof.

One way along the passage leads to Joanna and David's bedroom, which is where Fanny sleeps each night. The other way goes past a strange little room where David makes 'pictures' (somehow – I am not at all clear about this. It has something to do with his box on legs, I think. But it is a mystery). In this room he also 'writes letters' (which is something noisy he does with a machine and is another of the odd things he gets up to). His pictures, by the way, hang on the walls of the house. There's one of me and Bailey that I quite like – though it took ages for me to believe that was what it was and I still don't quite understand it. David told me it was a picture of us and I wanted to please him, so I wagged my tail and licked his hand. But what *is* a picture? That's what I didn't know. Is it a bit like what happens when you look into a still pool of water or a window when you can see yourself looking at yourself? (This is quite a trick. You have to look at the glass and not through it. The first time it happened to me, when I was just a young pup, I thought there was another dog outside the window and I got quite cross. Particularly when I noticed that everything I did the other stupid dog did as well. In the end I lost my temper and went for her. But she wasn't there of course, and I stubbed my nose on the glass instead and really hurt myself.)

The other room on the top floor was the sitting room. In winter, when it's cold, David sets fire to wood in a hole in the sitting-room wall. It's the best time of the year, I think. Sometimes the wind is really cold and the garden is all damp and dreary. But inside, by the fire, it's as warm as an autumn afternoon and I like nothing better than stretching out and dozing with the sound of the wood spitting and flaring and Fanny sleep-dreaming near me, while Joanna and David sit reading and listening to David's radio.

So, you see, I became a house dog at last and Bailey was a half house dog. And Fanny – well, I've never dared ask her, but I think she quite liked having us there as company. (Though we had to be very careful and not push ourselves forward. She always had to have her food first and there was never a suggestion that I should sleep on Joanna and David's bed or anything like that.)

The summer faded into a warm, golden autumn. There were fewer guests now and often we'd go off in the van for what Joanna called a 'picnic' – which is a trip with food. Actually, Bailey didn't always come with us. He said he'd rather spend the day chasing about up on Mel's campo. But really I don't think he ever took to riding in the van as much as I did. I noticed that he always shook a bit and kept his nose sticking out of the open window.

I think, because Bailey had lived longer in the wild than I had, that it was almost too late for him to settle down completely in a human house. He needed to be able to come and go. To be 'free', as he called it.

When the winter came and it was cold outside he still preferred sleeping on the porch. David built him a sort of big wooden box on its side – so that it had a front opening and a roof over his head. Even when it got very wintry – sometimes it poured with rain – he wouldn't come into the house. So David hung an old coat over the front opening of the box and I must admit that when I tried it out it was surprisingly snug inside.

'You do understand, don't you, Kitty?' Bailey begged, 'I like it because I can still get in and out. If there's anything I want to see in the night – if there's a sudden noise or a funny smell – then I just push past the coat and I'm free to go and look.'

I did wonder if he would have liked me to join him in the box. But he never said so and really, since I'd been ill and stayed at Vet's, I was a bit scared of being too much in the wild and was more than content to be inside and safe.

Joanna and David did go away that winter. But a guest came to stay and she fed us and looked after us. It was all right, but I was glad Fanny was there to reassure me. Otherwise I might have thought that Joanna and David had gone for good – which would have been awful. Joanna knows the best food and David knows the best walks and anyway the house is theirs and so it doesn't feel right when they're not in it.

As winter set in we all went away to the big water for three days. Bailey came too. It was so strange being back on a beach. It wasn't our beach. It was much further away; it took at least half a day in the van to get there.

Joanna and David and Fanny all stayed in a human house. But Bailey and I slept in the van. It was almost the best time I can ever remember. David left the window of the van open a bit and Bailey managed to wriggle in and out of it – so he didn't feel trapped. It was so good to be sleeping with him beside me once more and to feel his warm body next to mine and to hear his snuffling, yelping sleep-dreams. I decided that, come the good weather, I'd try and get Joanna to let me sleep out on the porch again. Of course I wouldn't feel afraid of the wild. Not with Bailey there to protect me. I think he liked having me there as well. He licked my ear a lot and sometimes, in his sleep, he would put a paw on my body.

One day while we were on the beach having a picnic Joanna and David gave each other 'presents'. (Things wrapped up in paper. The paper was good to play with.) Then they each gave Fanny a present. She got a rubber ball from David and a box of crunchy stuff to eat from Joanna.

(She didn't get to eat it all at once, and Bailey and I were given some of it. She only just didn't mind this. Well, she let Bailey have some, but she snapped at me when I took some from Joanna's hand.)

Then Bailey and I were each given a present.

As soon as Joanna opened the paper I knew that we were now their dogs. We were each given a house dog 'collar' – just like the one Fanny always wears. I think a collar is the final sign that a dog is a house dog. I'm not sure what they're for, but they mark you out as 'belonging' – if only because no dog in the wild would ever wear one. Apart from anything else, they'd be impossible for a dog to put on. You need a human's hands to manage it. (Unless, of course, the dog in the wild was on the run, then they might wear a collar. But that would be a sort of hangover from their previous life and wouldn't really count.)

My collar is green, like the trees and the plants, and Bailey's was blue, like the sky.

On the last day, on our way back from this present-giving trip, David stopped the van at our beach. He and Joanna went to the table place to eat some food and we were supposed to sit under the table with them. Fanny did. But Bailey and I trotted off after a while.

We looked for our first nest. But everything was different. Even the water channel had disappeared. There was a big round pipe there instead.

I went and found the yard where I'd been born. There were no dogs about, although later I did see one who gave me a questioning look. He could have been my brother, but if he was he didn't recognize me and I wasn't sure either.

It was so strange being back. It didn't seem possible that I had ever lived there. Even the big water was unfamiliar and I much preferred it on the beach where we'd spent the present-giving.

The only thing that now seems at all significant about being on the beach that day was watching Bailey looking up at the far horizon. He had his back to the big water and he was standing so tall that he seemed to be trying to fly as he strained for a better view. His eyes were alight and his tail was slowly flicking from side to side.

'Look, Kitty,' he whispered. 'Look at the high mountains.'

So I turned and saw the clear blue sky arching down over the yellow earth. I saw the wide valley rising up and the smudge of white and grey nestling in a fold of the land that I now knew was our village. And beyond, where the brown hills reached their upper limits, a thin band of cloud separated the earth from the fine cut-out edge of those far, high mountains. They seemed so distant and dreamlike; so unattainable. They were like a vision of another world, somewhere beyond anything we were ever likely to know. They were so unbelievably lovely; clean and sharp, thrusting up into that luminous sky, their peaks covered in glistening white that sparkled and flashed in the winter sunlight.

'Look at the snow,' Bailey sighed.

Chapter Twenty-Eight

The next bit is going to be hard to tell. It was harder still to live. Now, looking back, it seems almost unbelievable that so many important things could all happen on the same day.

It started when two visitors arrived at the house. They were humans that we'd often seen before. They lived in the village, I think. Fanny was quite fond of them.

It was one of those high spring days, with a warm sun when everything feels fresh and clean. A perfect day! It soon became clear that we were all going on a picnic together.

David asked Bailey if he wanted to come. But although he wagged his tail, he backed away.

'Oh, come! Please, Bailey!' I pleaded with him. I really wanted him to.

'No!' he said. 'There'll be too many humans in the car and it'll probably only be a picking trip.'

(Joanna and David sometimes go on picking trips. These are rather boring outings for us dogs. They drive off in the van until they find what they're looking for. Then they stop, get out and spend hours bending over, picking berries off plants and putting them into a bag. We just have to sit around and wait for them. The berries are small, like big seeds. I took one once, just to see what it was like. It tasted horrid. Joanna uses them when she is preparing human food, I think. But she never gives them to us to eat.)

So, in the end, we all went apart from Bailey.

That day David took a picture of Bailey in the wing mirror of the van. At least that's what he said he'd done, when Joanna and the other humans got in and we were driving off.

'I took a picture of Bailey in the wing mirror. He was sitting watching us going. I couldn't resist it.'

'Poor Bailey,' Joanna said, looking back, 'I wish he'd come as well.'

'He'll go up to Mel's campo for the day,' David said. 'He'll be all right.'

Oh, Bailey! Dearest Dog! You should have come! It was a long journey and you'd probably have trembled all the way but you'd have been so pleased in the end.

We went on a main road that was busy. Then we turned off onto narrow quiet lanes that wound up and down and eventually went right over the top of the brown hills. Down the other side, we reached a valley that I'd never seen before. We drove across this valley. We seemed to be going for miles and miles and I got a bit bored, if I'm honest. There is only so much fun to be got out of being in the van. The good thing is when you get to the end of the journey. The good thing is getting out and stretching and seeing where you are.

Then the ground started to get steeper as the lane wound upwards. I was wedged between the door and Joanna's leg and I'd been dozing. But the sound of the van engine grinding up the steep hills woke me up.

I got up and stretched. I gave Joanna's cheek a little lick and then I turned and looked out of the window. There were a lot of trees growing along the side of the lane and they blocked out the view. But I did notice that the air was much, much cooler.

I think I smelled the high mountains before I saw them. They have a particular sort of smell. It's the smell of a spring breeze, after rain. A sort of clean, new smell. If a smell could really smell of nothing, that's what it was like. Or everything! If a smell could contain every smell in the world, so that the smells each cancelled each other out – that's what the high mountains smelled of.

We pulled round a corner and the road got all bumpy. Then the thick wall of trees started to dwindle away. They grew less and less until there was only a last one, standing all on its own. I looked back at this tree and saw that the top of it was covered in white.

'We're here!' I heard David call and Fanny started to bark with excitement.

I turned back from looking at the tree and the light in front of me was so bright that I had to half shut my eyes.

'What is it, Fanny?' I yelped. 'What's happened to the ground?'

I couldn't understand it! It was as if all the colours of the earth had disappeared. Or maybe they hadn't yet arrived. Yes, that's it. It was as if the world was new or unfinished and the details were still waiting to be filled in.

'Come on!' Fanny barked, as David got out of the van and opened the door nearest to me. She was sitting in the middle of the seat, between Joanna and the lady visitor (her usual place), but she scrambled across Joanna and actually stepped on me – she was in such a hurry to get out.

I followed her more slowly. I wasn't at all sure about this strange, half-finished world that we'd come to.

As soon as I stepped out I felt an icy blast of breeze. It was so cold that it took my breath away and made me gasp. The air was so sharp and crisp that it crackled on my fur. The light was so dazzling that I couldn't, at first, look up into it.

'Where are we?' I gasped. 'What is this place?'

'Kitty!' David called and, as I turned towards him, he threw a handful of white powder at me. It broke on top of my head – and turned at once into ice-cold water. I lifted a paw and wiped it off my face, then I tasted it. It tasted of nothing.

'Kitty!' Joanna called and I turned towards her. She was holding her hand out. In it she was holding a pile of the white stuff. 'Come on!' she coaxed me. 'Come and play in the snow.'

The snow! Oh, Bailey! The snow! If only you'd come. If only you'd been there instead of me.

I sat down on the wet, cold ground and started to whimper. I couldn't bear that I was seeing snow and he wasn't there. I couldn't believe that he was missing his biggest dream.

'Oh, Bailey!' I howled.

'I don't think Kitty likes the snow!' the lady visitor said and she came and bent over me, to comfort me.

But I didn't want any human near me, not then. I had to be on my own. So I ran away a few steps until I was surrounded by the white, sparkling snow. Then I sat down again, curling my tail under me, and half turning my head away from them all. The land rose up in front of me; a sheet of white. Beyond the top of the nearest hill I could see more peaks and crags soaring up into the limitless blue sky.

'These are the mountains,' I said to myself. 'We're on the high mountains!'

I half closed my eyes and when I opened them again I believed, for an instant, that I could see Bailey. He was further up the hill and he was running away from me towards the distant peaks. He was barking and leaping and skipping through great drifts of flying, glittering snow.

'Bailey!' I barked and I started to chase after him.

But the snow was soft and deep and I found that my feet sank into it. It clung to my steps and made it difficult for me to move.

'Bailey!' I called again. Then I saw him stop and turn to look back at me. His tail was wagging and his eyes were bright. His tongue was peeping out of the side of his mouth and he looked so happy and so excited.

'Oh, Bailey!' I sobbed. 'Oh, Dog!' And then the vision vanished and he wasn't there any more.

Fanny loved the snow. She ran in it, scooping it up in her mouth and pushing her nose through it, so that it sprayed out in front of her. The humans walked about a bit and slapped their arms to keep themselves warm.

David took a lot of pictures with his box. I think that's maybe why we went there, so that he could have some snow pictures.

They tried to make me play with Fanny. They wanted to believe I was enjoying myself, I think. And I would have done – if only I hadn't been missing Bailey so much.

Then we all got back into the van and David drove away from the snow, back down the tree-lined road. We stopped where there was a huge, wide view of the sky and the earth. It must have been almost like flying, we were so high up. The humans had a picnic and Fanny and I were given special scraps.

Everyone was so jolly and merry. They'd all enjoyed seeing the snow, I suppose.

I tried to explain to Fanny why I felt so sad. But I don't think she understood.

'I expect we'll come again,' she said. 'Bailey can come with us next time.'

It was of course a sensible thing for her to say. So why didn't it comfort me? I looked back up the steep, tree-covered slope to where the tips of the mountains were still visible, white against the blue. It seemed so wrong that I'd come here before him — was that why I was sad?

Or did I know already? Had I actually for once seen into the future while I was regretting the present?

We were late getting back that night. It was after dark when David dropped the other humans near their house and then drove us up to the brown door.

'Bailey will be ravenous,' Joanna said, as she hurried up the path to the blue-water pool. 'Bailey,' she called, 'we're home.'

He wasn't there. He wasn't waiting under the porch. His box nest was empty.

'He must have been and gone,' David said. 'Maybe Mel has fed him.'

That had happened a few times. If Joanna and David were taking us off for a long day and Bailey wasn't coming, they'd tell Mel and he'd feed Bailey. It had happened before. And, once in a while, Bailey had gone off to explore and he hadn't come home. He'd once stayed out all night. It had all happened before.

But when he wasn't there the following morning I felt a cold shiver, like the snow breeze, go through me. David was worried as well. I knew he was. He tried to pretend otherwise. He didn't want to alarm us, I suppose.

'Dearest,' he called. 'I'll . . . just go and ask Mel . . .' And he hurried away down the path to the brown gate. I ran after him as far as the blue-water pool. But he told me to stay. He said he'd go on his own.

Joanna was in the kitchen. But she hadn't got music playing on David's radio. She usually had music playing. But this time the house was all silent.

Even Fanny seemed subdued. She was sitting in the wicker armchair. But she wasn't sleeping. She was listening and watching all the time.

'What is it?' I asked her. 'Why are they so . . . ?' I couldn't find the right word. I was going to say 'frightened', but then didn't dare to. I didn't want to hear the word, I suppose, because I didn't want to be frightened myself.

'They're remembering,' Fanny growled.

'What?'

She looked away from me. I thought she was going into one of her funny moods. I thought she was going to ignore me. For a moment I felt almost angry. I wanted her to comfort me. I wanted her to tell me . . .

'It's what happened to Boris,' she said. She was speaking to me, but she was looking away from me. Her voice was quite quiet. I had to really listen to hear what she was saying.

'I had four pups. Joanna and David found a good home for each of them. I thought I'd mind them going. But I didn't. Being a mother is very exhausting and I was quite tired by then. But one of them, one of the boys, he went to really nice people right here in this village. People we knew. So I went on seeing him. The people called him Boris and he was always coming up here to see me. Or, when David went down into the village, I'd go and see him. When Joanna and David went away, I'd go and stay with Boris. When Boris's humans went away, he'd come and stay here. He was my son. He was also my best friend. Joanna and David loved him as much as me, I think, and I never minded. And his humans loved me. I know they did . . .'

Her voice sort of petered out. She couldn't go on talking because I think she was remembering a great sadness. I waited for as long as I could. But I had such a cold, sharp pain in me.

'What happened?' I prompted her.

'We went for a walk – Joanna and David and Boris and me . . .' She paused again and then added, very quietly: 'He ate some poison – that's what they said.'

'What . . . what is "poison"?'

'It's stuff the farmers use. They put it down on the ground. They hide it in corn, or bits of meat; it's always covered in something tasty. The rats and the foxes go for this food and, as the poison is mixed up with it, they eat it as well.'

'What does it do?'

'It kills any animal that swallows it. Not only foxes. Not only rats. All animals; and birds, I expect. Of course . . .' Her voice broke again, then she continued in a shaky whisper, 'It kills dogs as well.' She shook her head. She was trembling and sobbing. But I had to make her go on. I had to know.

'How?' I yelped. 'How do they die? I must know, Fanny. You must tell me.'

'They suffer horribly and die in agony. Their bodies go all stiff. There's a stink in the air of everything that's foul. It's the smell of . . . human evil.'

In my memory I suddenly see Bailey trotting ahead of me along a narrow path between high grasses. I see him stop and pull back. I run up to stand beside him. What is it that I'm remembering? Where are we? And then I smell that terrible, human-made, plastic-sharp, acid, never-going-away stench that I've only ever smelled once before. And I remember at once the dead fox down in the green valley, on the day that we first reached our scrape-nest. I remember its poor tortured body and the flies buzzing round its open mouth.

'Bailey!' I shriek.

After three nights Joanna and David gave up hope. We'd searched the country all round the village. Mel did as well. I made them take me to the scrape-nest every evening. But he was never there and I always knew he would have been if he could have walked, or staggered or crawled.

On the fourth day, in the morning, David and I went down to the green valley one last time. I stood on the bluff of rock by the first trees and barked his name.

'Dog! Dog! Dog!' I cried. I was shaking with grief and anger and pity. 'DOG!' I howled — a long, echoing, almost endless sound.

David came and kneeled down beside me then. He picked me up and pressed his face into my back. I could feel the wet of his tears soaking through my fur.

It helped me to know that he missed him as well; that it was hurting for him also. It did help — to share the pain.

Chapter Twenty-Nine

And perhaps that should have been the end of the story. But it isn't.

Bryn has come to stay again. It's ages since he was last here, when I was ill and lost our puppies. That means he hasn't been here for almost three years.

It's two years since Bailey went away.

We never did find his body, so we never really knew what happened. Joanna and David have always believed that he was poisoned. The farmers had been putting poison down to keep the foxes off the partridge eggs. (The farmers like to shoot the partridges.) I think it upset David terribly that he never could find Bailey's body.

I've never been certain about the poison idea, myself. But of course, I was the only one who saw him racing through the snow up on the high mountain that day – the day he disappeared. I've never mentioned this to Fanny. I think I've always been afraid that, if I did, she might not believe me and that her disbelief would somehow take him away from me.

Because it does help me to think that he went off on an adventure. I suppose a bit of me hopes that he might come back, you see. Or at least that one day we'll be together again. I imagine us running side by side through the snow, laughing and barking. He jumps at me, nipping my neck and licking my ear. The breeze is so cool and the light so brilliant. And we are as happy as we ever were. That's how I want it to be. That's the dream that keeps me going.

I didn't think I could survive without him. But I have. Life continues in the magic garden. The seasons come and go. So do the guests. It is just that half of me has disappeared.

But, you know, he was never cut out to be a house dog and he made so many sacrifices for me. He always wanted me to be safe – he really knew what it was like, living in the wild. But he didn't want to be safe himself. He wanted to be free.

Well, I'm sure he is free now.

I don't mean to be sad. I'm past sadness now. Really, I have a very happy life. Truly, I do. It's only that Bryn coming back after so long has made me remember, that's all.

We all went for a walk yesterday and we saw the stray. Oh, I should have mentioned – a new stray dog has arrived in the village. Both Fanny and I like him a lot. He doesn't look like Bailey – he's taller and he's a sort of dirty white colour all over. But he has the same bright eyes and when his tail wags he really seems so full of life – though, poor creature, he's half starved. I think what I'm saying is that he's got Bailey's spirit, and that's what attracts me to him.

We've got him to follow us home a few times and I'm sure Joanna and David are both aware of him. But of course Bryn is the one who could get things moving. At the end of the walk yesterday he kneeled down and stroked him – which was a very good sign.

The stray was a bit doubtful about being stroked. But I ran up and sniffed him. 'Go on,' I told him. 'It's quite safe.'

'What would you know?' the stray growled. 'You're a house dog.'

I smiled to myself. But I didn't say anything.

I think, by the smell of him, he's probably about a year old. And he's certainly been living wild for most of that time. He has that strong stench of dirt and fear. I recognized it at once. It used to be our smell – Bailey's and mine.

When we reached the brown door he was still following us. He trots along at a safe distance and always has one of his front paws turned sideways – as if he's ready to spring away to safety at the first hint of danger.

'He needs food,' Bryn said, looking back at him.

'I'll put some out for him tonight,' Joanna said, going into the garden and calling to Fanny and me to follow her.

'If you wait,' I barked, running back to the stray, 'the humans will bring you scraps.'

'Why?' he asked.

'I don't know,' I replied. 'Because they're kind. Some humans are.'

'Oh, just look at him!' Bryn called to David, who was waiting for us all to go ahead of him through the door.

'Don't start that again!' David said with a laugh. Then he looked back at the stray. 'He looks bald – like a golf ball.'

'No, he doesn't,' Bryn said, kneeling down and holding out a hand to the stray. 'His hair's all matted, that's all. He just needs a good wash.'

'He certainly needs a good feed.' David said thought-fully. 'Don't you, boy? You want some good nourishing food.

Sputnik! That's what he reminds me of! He has the sleek look of an orbiting satellite.'

'Well, you keep orbiting round here, old chap!' Bryn whispered. 'It's a good pull-in for strays.'

'Sputnik!' David called and the stray wagged his tail.

Sputnik! I don't know how David thinks of the names. Evidently Bailey was the name of another human who took pictures with a little box – like David does. That's what I heard David say once to someone who asked. He called Dog Bailey because he was black and white – like the pictures out of the little box are black and white. That's what he said, anyway. And evidently I am called Kitty because when Joanna first saw me she thought I was a cat. A cat! Would you believe it? Apparently another name for a cat is kitty. I am named after a cat. I hate cats!

But I must tell the stray how important it is for them to give him a name. Start by getting a name, I shall say. Then get scraps. Then, if you're lucky, you'll get inside the brown door. Once you've got that far, take it very gently. A little at a time. Don't be over-eager. Don't push in. Let them get used to you. Oh, and make a point of getting on with Fanny. Fanny is very important. If Fanny likes you, that is a very good sign. If, after that, you see David taking your picture you're over halfway there. Finally they may give you a collar. The day that happens, you can relax. You'll know you're home.

Sputnik! Fanny says it'll be good to have a male about the house again. She says she thinks he's a good-looking dog – for a stray.

I admit he does seem more than average. I do like that light in his eyes. And he has the scent of adventure about him. He has no doubt been through quite a lot. Won't he be surprised when he hears about us?

Yes, I'll probably grow to be fond of him.

But he'll never take the place of Bailey. Not for me. Not in my heart. Once you've known a dog like Bailey, all the others must always be second best.

I might even get used to calling him Sputnik – stupid name!

I did end up calling Bailey, Bailey.

But in my heart he was always just Dog.